FIGHTING RANGER

Travis Logan, a Texas Ranger, is heading for Alder Creek when big trouble comes over a ridge, in the shape of a woman being chased by two killers. Pledged to fight lawlessness, Logan goes into action, and is engulfed by the trouble he searches out. The odds are greatly stacked against him; and when hot lead starts flying, they won't improve until Logan untangles a web of deceit, and stamps his particular brand of law and order on the greedy, callous men who stand in his way . . .

CORBA SUNMAN

FIGHTING RANGER

Complete and Unabridged

LINFORD
Leicester

First published in Great Britain in 2016 by
Robert Hale
an imprint of The Crowood Press
Wiltshire

First Linford Edition
published 2019
by arrangement with
The Crowood Press
Wiltshire

A catalogue record for this book is available
from the British Library.

ISBN 978–1–4448–4110–7

Published by
F. A. Thorpe (Publishing)
Anstey, Leicestershire

Set by Words & Graphics Ltd.
Anstey, Leicestershire
Printed and bound in Great Britain by
T. J. International Ltd., Padstow, Cornwall

This book is printed on acid-free paper

1

Travis Logan halted his dusty buckskin when he reached a fork in the trail he was riding to Alder Creek, West Texas. Covered in dust and unshaven, his keen blue eyes swivelled under his hat brim, instinctively checking his surroundings, and a frown appeared on his lean features, for the rolling echoes of a rifle shot were sounding from his right. His expression hardened as he listened, thinking he was the target. As a Texas Ranger, he was an aiming mark for every badman in Texas. He had been a Ranger four years, and right now he was on his way to Alder Creek because there was trouble to be handled.

His bronzed face was taut as he listened to the fading echoes of the shot, and when a rider suddenly appeared on a low ridge he reached for his Winchester 4.40 and jacked a shell into the breech. The rider was coming hell for leather, long black hair streaming out, and Logan's teeth clicked together when he realized he was looking at a woman. She came hammering down the slope, pushing her mount with hands and heels, and as she drew nearer he could see she was crying, mouth agape, face contorted in panic and shock. Her cheeks were wet with tears.

When she saw Logan she shied away to keep at a safe distance, and then changed her mind and came towards him, raising dust. Logan thought she intended riding him down and swung his horse out of her path. But she hauled on her reins and her mount raised dust as it came to a slithering halt only a couple of feet from him.

'What's your hurry, ma'am?' Logan demanded. His big frame was coiled, ready for action, his mouth a thin slit under a snub nose; brown eyes set deeply under frowning brows. He was wearing a grey store suit and a white shirt with a black shoelace tie around his neck. Broad-shouldered, his lean waist was encircled by crossed gunbelts, each containing a Colt .45. He looked mean and dangerous.

The woman was drooping in her saddle, sobbing unrestrainedly. He took in her appearance at a glance; red divided skirt, a white blouse, calf-length riding boots, no hat. She was a handsome woman despite her agitation. Her eyes were cornflower blue. Her shoulders heaved as she gasped for breath, and he waited patiently until she could speak.

When she produced a handkerchief to dab at her eyes, Logan asked her: 'What's your name, ma'am?'

'I'm Dinah Shadde,' she gasped. 'My husband, Cole, owns the Circle S just beyond that ridge.'

'I'm Travis Logan, Mrs Shadde, of the Texas Rangers.'

Behind her, on the ridge, two riders appeared, their movement attracting

Logan's gaze. One of them was holding a rifle in his left hand. When the man reined in and shifted the rifle into a shooting position, Logan reached out, grabbed the woman's reins, and spurred his horse into a long depression to his right. As they moved into cover he heard the crack of a shot, and a slug kicked up dust on the rim of the depression.

'Who are those two men back there?' he demanded. 'Why are they shooting at you?'

'They shot my husband! Four men rode into our ranch and shot my husband in cold blood. He wasn't even carrying a gun. I was in the house, looking out the window, and when Cole fell I ran out the back door and jumped on his horse to make a run to town for help. Two of the men followed, shooting at me. Please help me!'

'Stay in cover.' Logan gigged his horse forward until he could peer up the slope.

The riders were galloping down off

the ridge, coming towards the depressions, firing shots to gain the initiative. Logan heard slugs thumping into the sun-baked ground. He dismounted, trailed his reins, and lifted his Winchester, the butt settling in his right shoulder and his left eye closing. He drew a bead on the right-hand man and squeezed the trigger. The long gun recoiled and Logan opened his left eye to observe. The rider reared back as the slug smacked into his breastbone, his hands convulsively snatching on his reins. His horse whirled to the right and he lost his balance; pitched out of the saddle.

The other rider increased his shooting. Logan took aim and fired again. The sharp smell of gunsmoke whipped back into his face and he wrinkled his nose. The man slumped over the neck of his horse, dropped his gun, and was carried past the depression by the galloping horse, gradually slipping sideways in his saddle until he sprawled out of leather and bounced on the ground.

Logan regained his feet. He went back to where Mrs Shadde was holding the horses and slid his rifle into the saddle-boot.

'It's okay now,' he said laconically. 'We'd better get to your place and check on your husband.'

She swung into her saddle and led out, silent, her face frozen, blue eyes like stones from a creek bottom. Logan followed her up to the top of the ridge and, as they plunged down the reverse slope, he spotted a ranch house in the distance. He ranged up alongside her.

'Let's take it easy,' he advised. 'You said there were four men.'

She nodded, but continued, and they approached the ranch, swept through the gate, and went on to the house. Logan saw a man sprawled in front of the porch, and a movement inside the house, at a window overlooking the yard, caught his attention. He drew his right-hand pistol and shouted a warning to Mrs Shadde.

'Stop and take cover,' he called.

She ignored him, her eyes on her fallen husband. She reined in beside the prone man and slid out of the saddle to drop to her knees beside him. Logan, watching the house intently, saw further movement beyond the window. He raised his pistol when a pane of glass suddenly shattered; he caught the glint of sunlight on metal, and fired a shot at the bearded face peering out at him. Gunsmoke flared, and the crash of the shot flung a string of echoes across the yard. The face disappeared from the window. Simultaneously, a man came diving out through the open doorway to the left, landed on the boards of the porch, and rolled a couple of times before coming up on one knee. He was holding a Colt .45 in his right hand.

Logan, hair-triggered, snapped a shot that smacked into the man's chest. The man threw down his gun and flattened out on his face. His left leg kicked convulsively a couple of times before he relaxed.

'Stay where you are,' Logan called to

Mrs Shadde, his eyes and attention on the front of the house. 'I'll check around. How's your husband?'

'He's alive! But he's bad hurt!'

'I'll be back in a moment.' Logan stepped on to the porch. A sideways glance informed him that the man on the porch was dead. He went into the house fast, ducking to one side as he crossed the threshold, the muzzle of his gun weaving. There was a man lying on the floor by the window with the broken pane — gun discarded. Logan crossed to him and kicked his leg to get a response. The man did not move. He had taken Logan's slug in his face.

Logan checked through the house. It was deserted. He peered down at the yard from an upper window and saw Mrs Shadde still kneeling beside her husband. He thudded down the stairs, spurs tinkling musically, and went out to her side. She had her husband's head in her lap. Cole Shadde was uncon-scious. There was blood on his chest.

'Let me look at him.' Logan dropped

to one knee beside Mrs Shadde. She had unbuttoned her husband's shirt, and opened it to reveal a bullet hole in the right side of the chest some three inches below the collar bone. 'It's serious,' he said. 'Get some water and something to bandage him. I'll stop the bleeding and then we'd better get him into Alder Creek. I expect there's a doctor in the town. I don't think his life is in danger; I know about things like that.'

'Doc Keeble is in town,' she replied, getting to her feet.

She ran into the house; reappeared moments later carrying a bowl of water and some linen. When Logan offered to attend to Shadde she shook her head.

'I trained as a nurse before I married,' she said.

'I'll take a look at those men while you get your wagon ready to take Cole to town.' Logan went to the man sprawled on the porch, checked his pockets; found nothing but a few dollars and the odds and ends that men accumulate over a period of time. He went into the house, used a small mat to cover the dead man's head — he had taken a bullet in his forehead and was lying in a pool of blood — and dragged him out to the yard.

He returned to Mrs Shadde. She was now looking easier, and smiled wanly when she spoke.

'I think Cole will be all right but he badly needs a doctor. Can we go to town now? I can hitch the horses to the wagon.'

'Put some straw in the bottom. I'd like to take the dead men along.'

She nodded and hurried off to the barn. Logan stood in the yard looking around. The ranch was small but well run. The buildings were in good repair. A fair-sized herd was grazing in the distance. Cole Shadde had obviously put in a lot of hard toil, and now he was lying on his back in the dust of his yard with a bullet in him; shot by a hard-case that probably hadn't done an honest day's work in his life.

Mrs Shadde brought a wagon from the rear of the house. Logan loaded the two dead hardcases first.

'Take a look at them,' Logan said. 'Tell me if you've seen either of them before. I'm wondering why four men rode in here and shot your husband for no apparent reason.'

She looked at the men and shook her head.

'I haven't seen either of them before,' she said firmly.

Logan covered the two figures with some straw and then they lifted her husband carefully and placed him in the back of the wagon.

'You'd better get in with him and I'll tie my horse behind,' he said. 'I'll drive to town.'

'I'll stay in town until Cole is out of the wood,' she said. 'I'd better get some things I might need.'

Logan nodded and tied his horse to the wagon. He stood patting the horse until Mrs Shadde appeared from the house, loaded with a case and an armful of clothes. When she had settled in the wagon beside her husband Logan got into the driving seat and they set out for Alder Creek. They reached the scene of the initial shooting and Logan collected the other two dead men, pitched them into the wagon like a couple sacks of grain, and covered them with straw. They continued.

The trail took them straight to town, and Logan was alert for further trouble as they rode. He had been told by his superior to expect to find lawlessness — there had been reports of rustling — but cold-blooded murder of lawful men going about their normal everyday life was extreme, and Logan wondered what was going on, and what the local law was doing about it.

Alder Creek was a small cow town. Most of the buildings fronting Main Street were adobe. Mrs Shadde directed him to the doctor's house, and by the time they reached it Logan had spotted the sheriff's office across the street beside a brick-built bank.

Mrs Shadde ran into the doctor's office while Logan unfastened the tailboard and stood looking around the street. The town seemed quiet. There was a buckboard in front of the general store being loaded with provisions, and a stage coach was standing in front of the stage depot. A couple of men were seated on tip-tilted chairs on the boardwalk in front of a saloon.

Mrs Shadde returned, followed by a short, fleshy man of about fifty, who was dressed in shirt sleeves and grey pants. His black hair was thinning on top and greying at the temples. He had a careworn face, and dark eyes that were dull, as if his way of life had disappointed him over the passing years.

Logan introduced himself, giving only his name, and Doc Keeble shook hands and turned away abruptly to examine Cole Shadde.

'I think he'll be fine,' said Keeble shortly. 'Give me a hand to get him into my office, Logan.'

Between them they lifted Shadde and took him into the house, where he was laid on a couch in the doctor's office. Logan departed immediately but paused at the door to speak to Mrs Shadde.

'I'm going across to the sheriff's office,' he told her. 'I'll be back shortly. Do you have any friends in town you can stay with while you're here?'

She nodded. 'I shall be all right now. Thank you for saving my life. Those men intended on killing me.' She spoke in a low tone that carried a great deal of stress.

'I'm glad I was around,' he replied, and departed.

The sheriff's office across the street was adobe-built. The street door stood wide open, and Logan could see a shirt-sleeved man sitting at a desk inside; elbows on the desk his head lowered, resting comfortably on his cupped hands. Logan paused and glanced around the street. He saw a rider entering the town, mounted on a grey horse. The newcomer reined it at a hitch rail in front of the saloon a block away and dismounted. He paused to look around, and for a moment he studied Logan's motionless figure curiously. Then his gaze shifted to the wagon in front of the doctor's office. He swung back into his saddle and came along the street to rein in beside the wagon, ignoring Logan's presence.

Logan remained motionless, watching. The newcomer, a man aged around thirty, was wearing range clothes — denims, a red shirt, yellow neckerchief tied loosely around his neck, and a black Stetson pulled down low over his eyes. He was powerfully built, and had a pistol strapped around his waist. His face was rugged and wore a hard expression that underlined the fact that he should not to be approached unless necessary.

The man leaned forward in his saddle, peering closely at the loose straw in the back of the wagon. Logan

15

walked back across the street towards him. The man heard his boots and glanced over his shoulder. He dropped his right hand to his holstered gun when he saw Logan.

'You seem almighty interested in the wagon,' observed Logan sharply.

'Hell, yes. There's blood on that straw. Who brought the wagon into town? And it's standing outside the doc's office; has someone been hurt?'

'Who are you?' Logan countered.

'I'm Ben Wadham. You're a stranger. Who in hell are you?'

'The name is Travis Logan; Texas Ranger.'

'The hell you say! Waal, Logan, there is a whole heap of trouble in this county. I hope for your sake you ain't come single-handed.'

'I'm alone — there's only one heap of trouble, so I heard.' Logan's eyes sparkled momentarily. 'What do you do around here?'

'My pa, Sam Wadham, bought a cow spread a few miles out, to the north.

We've been here six months; came down from Kansas. But we didn't figure on getting a double handful of trouble, and we don't need a Ranger nosing in. We'll handle this trouble in our own way. Who brought this wagon in?'

'I drove it in from the Shadde ranch. Cole Shadde is in the doc's office getting patched up. His wife is with him. I happened along in time to save Mrs Shadde from being gunned down. That's real trouble, and I'm handling it and anything else that is going on around here.'

'Who shot Shadde?'

'That's enough questions.' Logan turned to go on to the sheriff's office, but after a couple of strides he turned back and spoke to Wadham. 'It sounds as if you're involved in the trouble. How did you get caught up in it?'

'It was already here, just waiting for us to show up. In the first place we were hit by rustlers, but it'll end in a big blow-up, and we'll be riding high when that happens.'

Logan continued, and as he stepped on to the sidewalk in front of the law office a man appeared in the doorway. He was around forty-five, of powerful build with wide shoulders. His blue eyes were keen and he had curly brown hair. He wore a grey store suit, an open-neck white shirt, and riding boots. A gunbelt around his waist held a holster on his right hip containing a .45 Peacemaker Colt. A sheriff's star glinted on the front of his shirt.

'What's going on out here?' the lawman demanded. He gazed keenly at Logan. 'You're a stranger. When did you get into town?'

'I've just arrived. I'm Travis Logan, Texas Ranger.' Logan gave a terse explanation of what had happened out at the Shadde ranch, and saw shock spread across the lawman's hard features.

'So it's started,' he said, shaking his head. 'I've been expecting it to flare — it's been smouldering a long time.

I'm glad to know you, Logan. I got a wire from your headquarters last week, saying that a Ranger was on his way. I'm Abe Deacon, county sheriff. Let's take a look at the men you killed. If I do know any of them it could lead us to the gang behind our trouble.'

They walked across the street and the sheriff climbed into the back of the wagon. Logan stood watching. He glanced around the street. Ben Wadham was nowhere in sight — his horse was standing hip-shot at the hitch rail in front of the saloon. Deacon uncovered the bodies, and an exclamation ripped from him as he gazed at the blood-stained corpses.

'Do you know any of them?' Logan demanded.

Deacon shook his head as he climbed out of the wagon. 'I've seen a couple of them around town, but they don't show up very often.'

'We need to talk,' Logan said tersely. 'You can give me the background to this trouble.'

'Sure thing, but I'd better get a statement from Mrs Shadde first. Wait in my office. I'll bring Mrs Shadde over here.'

'My job is more important,' Logan cut in, 'and I need to get started on it. Give me ten minutes and then I'll start investigating. I'll keep in touch with you, and I'll call on you for help if I find more trouble than I can handle.'

Deacon nodded and turned back to his office. Logan followed, and when Deacon dropped into his seat behind the desk Logan sat down on a corner of it, one foot swinging.

'There's been a run of trouble — rustling, robbery and the like,' said Deacon heavily. 'Not much to start with but it's got a whole lot worse. I've got suspicions, but I'll keep them to myself for the moment. I'd like you to make your own decision about what's going on.'

Logan shook his head. 'Tell me all you know,' he said sharply.

'A man called Sam Wadham moved

into the old Swain spread to the north of town. His brand is SW. He's got half a score of men who are real salty hardcases — brought them with him from Kansas. The present trouble seemed to pick up after he came on the range.'

'I met Ben Wadham out by the wagon before you came out to the street,' Logan said. 'I guess the SW spread will do for me to start an investigation. Are there any trouble-makers in town?'

'Yeah, there are always a few hanging around in any town — men who don't work but always seem to have money in their pockets. They gather in McSween's saloon — Bull McSween is a real hardcase.' Deacon scratched his chin. 'But I can't let you ride out without mentioning Frank Harland, who owns the Tented H. He's got the biggest spread in the county and a tough outfit to back him. There are six trigger men in his crew who don't do anything but watch for trouble, and backbone. His top gun is Smack Morgan, a bullying type who sells muscle as well as gun speed.'

'It sounds like I'll have my work cut out,' Logan mused, making a mental note of the names he had been given. 'Give me details for getting to Tented H. I'll go there first.'

'I'll tell you this: if you're caught riding on Tented H grass you'll never ride off it alive,' said Deacon harshly. 'Don't think your badge will protect you. That bunch out there ain't got a lick of respect for the law, either yours or mine.'

'Thanks for the warning, Sheriff.' Logan stood up and moved to the door. He paused and looked at the worried-looking lawman. 'I've been doing my job for a long time now, and I've met all kinds. I sleep easy at night because I don't think about what I do or count the odds against me. I take life one day at a time. The men I fight know all the tricks, and until now I've managed to best them, and I'll go on like this until I do meet the one who is faster than me. I'll draw against anyone who wants to try his luck because that's my job. I'll head out to Tented H now and talk to Frank Harlan. See you later.'

He stepped out of the office on to the boardwalk and paused to look around. His eyes narrowed into slits when he glanced across the street and saw Mrs Shadde standing outside the doctor's office. She was being confronted by a man who had hold of her right elbow, and she was struggling to get free of his grasp . . .

2

Logan ran across the street. Mrs Shadde heard his feet and looked up, her face expressing extreme fear as she tried to get away from the man. She cried out when she recognized Logan.

'Help me!' she cried. 'He wants me to go with him.'

The man turned as Logan reached the sidewalk. He was tall and thin, dressed like a cowpuncher, and wore a gun tied down low on his right hip. His face was harsh, his brown eyes hard and glittering. He looked Logan up and down and sneered.

'Butt out,' he said in a fierce tone. 'Get the hell out or I'll gut shoot you!'

'What do you want with Mrs Shadde?' Logan demanded.

The man reached for his holstered gun. Logan threw a right-hand punch that thudded against the man's chin and his left hand reached out to secure a grip on the man's gun as it cleared its holster. The weapon dragged out of leather as the man fell backwards, and Logan took possession of it as he watched the man's progress. The hardcase fell on the sidewalk and flattened out on his back. He was motionless for several moments, and then came surging to his feet as his brain cleared from the effects of Logan's punch.

Logan threw a second punch that crushed the man's nose. Blood spurted. The man dropped to his knees. Logan hit him across the left temple with the barrel of the pistol he was holding, and the man stretched out on the boardwalk once more and relaxed. Mrs Shadde had fallen back against the wall of the doctor's house, a hand to her mouth. Her face was pale and she was trembling. Logan glanced around and saw the sheriff emerge from his office and come hurrying across the street.

What happened?' Logan asked Mrs Shadde.

'I came out of the doctor's office to go to the sheriff's office, and this man was standing on the street.'

Sheriff Deacon arrived, breathing heavily. He gazed down at the unconscious man and then looked at Logan.

'What happened?' he asked. Logan let Mrs Shadde answer.

Deacon shook his head. He bent over the fallen man and shook him by the shoulder.

'Come on, Johnson, snap out of it,' he said loudly.

'You know him?' Logan asked.

'I sure do.' Deacon spoke in a stilted manner, his lips twisting. 'He's Tip Johnson, one of Frank Harland's Tented H gun-hands.' He glanced at Mrs Shadde. 'Did he say what he wanted with you, ma'am?'

She shook her head mutely. Logan could see she was beyond making a reply. He bent over Johnson and shook him with some force. The man's head rolled on his shoulders, but his eyelids flickered, and Logan shook him again. Johnson groaned and his eyes opened. Logan hauled him to his feet.

'Let's get him into your office and question him, Sheriff,' Logan said.

Deacon nodded and took hold of Johnson's other arm, and they walked him across the street. Deacon called to Mrs Shadde to follow them. They entered the office and Deacon thrust Johnson into a seat by the desk.

'Okay, so what have you got to say, Johnson?' said Deacon harshly. 'Why were you accosting Mrs Shadde?'

'I wasn't. I heard what happened to Cole Shadde and I wanted to help her.' Johnson fingered his jaw, which was beginning to swell.

'When I saw you she was struggling to get away from you,' Logan said. 'Let's have the truth, huh?'

Johnson regarded him with a harsh gaze. 'Who in hell are you, mister? How'd you come to push your long nose into this? I'll look you up when I get out of here.'

'I've got a pretty good notion to take you outside and teach you some manners,' Logan said.

Johnson laughed sneeringly. 'Go up against me and you take on the whole Tented H crew. Do you wanta die young?'

'You talk big,' Logan countered, 'but you don't have any of your crew behind you right now. Put a curb on your tongue or you'll find yourself in real trouble. What were your intentions towards Mrs Shadde?'

'I've told you once.' Johnson shook his head. 'I don't grind my coffee twice, mister.'

'Johnson, you better put a stop to your gab or I'll forget I'm the sheriff and put a knot in your tongue,' Deacon said. 'If I catch you bothering Mrs Shadde again I'll toss you in the jug and hit you with so many charges you'll spend the next five years behind bars. Go on, get outa here before I change my mind and put a fence around you.'

Johnson got up, grinning, and went to the street door. He paused and threw a backward glance at Logan. 'I'll see you through gunsmoke,' he snarled.

'Johnson, get out. Climb on your horse and ride back to Tented H. Don't let me see you back inside of town limits again or you'll be seeing *me* through gunsmoke.' Deacon breathed heavily, his patience gone.

'Any time you fancy your chance,' said Johnson with a smirk. He went out to the street and they heard the sound of his boots fading on the boardwalk.

Deacon sighed and shook his head. 'I can see that I'll have to tighten up my law dealing,' he mused. 'No one's got any respect for me now. I must be getting old, I guess. I can remember the time when I wouldn't permit a two-bit gun-hand to come within a mile of the decent folk living here. Now the town is filled with trash and saddle scum.'

'There'll be a difference around here after I start operating,' Logan promised. 'You take care of Mrs Shadde until her trouble is settled, Sheriff, and I'll get moving. I'll make for Tented H first and take a look around, and then I'll do the same at the Wadham place.'

'Just be careful on the range,' Deacon warned. 'You got the directions straight for Tented H?'

'I have. See if you can get some identification on any of those four men I shot. I'll see you later.' Logan went to depart, but paused in the doorway and looked back at Mrs Shadde. 'I'll check on you when I get back to town,' he told her, and she nodded.

He smiled reassuringly at her and stepped out on to the sidewalk. Sheriff Deacon followed him and paused in the doorway. A loaded freight wagon was moving along the street, pulled by a four-horse hitch. The wagon driver met Logan's gaze with piercing brown eyes, which stayed on him as the wagon rolled past the law office. The driver was huge, about six foot six, Logan guessed, and there was something about him that sent a spark of recognition through Logan's brain.

He frowned as the wagon went on. The driver continued to look at Logan over his shoulder. He was wearing a red shirt and a brown leather vest. The twin muzzles of a double-barrelled shotgun pointed skywards, leaning against the brake handle of the wagon. The face turned toward Logan was rugged, set in a cold expression, and Logan searched his mind for memories of having met the man some place before.

'Who is that wagon driver?' Logan said.

'Jake Larter,' Deacon replied. 'He owns the freighting business around here; him and his partner Tom Barden. You never know where Larter is gonna show up. He'll go anywhere and haul anything if there's a profit to be made.' Deacon glanced at Logan's face, read his expression, and asked, 'Do you know him from somewhere?'

'I've got a feeling I've seen him before, but I can't place him at the moment.'

'He sure stands out in a crowd.' Deacon turned and went back into his office.

Logan started for his horse and a sudden movement to his right caught his eye. He turned his head and saw Tip Johnson waiting only feet away in the mouth of the alley beside the law office. Johnson was unsmiling, his face a cold mask of murderous intention. His right hand was hovering above the butt of his holstered gun.

'There's no time like the present, punk,' Johnson grated. 'I'm gonna teach you not to stick your nose into my business. Pull your gun!'

'Hold your horses,' said Logan quickly. His right hand was down at his side, the butt of his holstered pistol touching the inside of his wrist. 'I'm a Texas Ranger. I don't draw on any man unless he draws first. I'm here on law business, and any fighting I do will be for the law.'

'A Texas Ranger?' Johnson's lips pulled tight against his teeth, but indecision showed momentarily in his eyes. 'The hell you say! I got some friends who'll be interested in that news.' He eased his hand away from his gun butt and his face relaxed, his expression changing as the desire to kill seeped out of him. 'I'll see you some other time, mister.'

'You ride for Tented H,' Logan said.

'That ain't any of your business.' Johnson's hand slid toward his gun butt again, but he changed his mind once more and turned away.

Logan watched the gunman's progress along the sidewalk. Johnson reached the saloon and pushed through the batwings. Logan went to his horse and swung into the saddle. He rode along the street and moved out of town, following the trail north. The sheriff's instructions for reaching the Tented H were sharp in his mind as he pushed his mount into a lope and went on steadily.

Two hours later he reined in on a ridge and looked down at the Tented H ranch located in a valley. The ranch house was set apart from the barn and cook shack, and was a single-storey building with a porch along its front. There was a big corral to the right, and a bunk house was located nearby. A man armed with a rifle was standing at the gate to the yard, and there was a wrangler working in the corral, breaking in a horse. Dust was flying and the shouts of the man at work echoed across the range. A stream meandered down the valley, widened into a creek near the house, and then continued as a narrower stream further down the valley.

Logan rode down from the ridge and approached the gate. The guard straightened from an indolent attitude and took hold of his rifle with both hands. He eyed Logan suspiciously as he rode up, and lifted a hand, palm outward, to stop him. Logan intended riding on to the house without stopping.

'Hold up there.' The guard was tall

and broad, and didn't look like a ranch-hand. He had a mean expression on his face. Twin pistols were holstered on crossed belts around his waist, and he seemed eager to shoot someone. 'What in hell do you think I'm standing here for?' he demanded.

'I'm here to see Frank Harlan,' Logan said patiently. 'I've ridden out from town to see him, so let me pass or take me to him.'

'What's your business?'

'That's between Harlan and me.'

'You can ride in. But I'll be watching you all the way to the porch. Don't try to get smart and duck off the trail before you get to the house. I can hit anything I shoot at.'

Logan shook his head and rode on. He crossed the yard and reined up in front of the porch. There was a movement at the window to the right of the door, which was half open. Logan sat his mount, waiting for a reaction from the house, and a moment later a man stepped into view, thrusting the door wide as he filled the aperture. He was tall and powerful; moved with the assurance of one who had all the confidence in the world at his finger-tips. He was dressed in range clothes — a blue shirt, denims, and a black Stetson pushed back on his wide forehead. His eyes were brown, and they were filled with a harsh expression as he looked intently at Logan. His thin-lipped mouth was taut, turned down slightly at the corners as if he were naturally bad-tempered. He wore a pistol low down on his right hip and his hand was close to the butt.

'Who in hell are you, mister, and whaddya want, coming into my yard?' He looked past Logan and gazed around. 'Did that damn fool Bronson let you in? And how did you ride across my grass without getting yourself shot? What's the matter with my gun crew? I pay them top wages and they can't do their job properly.' He came out to the porch and looked towards the bunk house. 'Hey, Morgan, where in hell are you?' he yelled, his voice echoing faintly. 'Get over here and do your job. What the hell do I pay you for?'

Logan remained motionless in his saddle. He looked towards the bunk house, and his lips pulled in tightly against his teeth when a man emerged from the low building.

'What do you want, Harlan?' the man called. 'Can't a man get any peace around this damn place? I was out riding all night, so don't call for me until I'm good and ready to show my face. What the hell do you want? You damn well woke me up.'

'I'll tell you what I want. Just do what I pay you for. Bronson is standing guard on the gate and he's let a stranger ride in here carrying a gun. Is that what you call good protection? I could have been shot a dozen times while you were in your sack. Get over here and tell me what's going on.'

Morgan started across to the house, and Logan took note of him. The gun crew boss was no taller than six feet but his width almost matched his height. He was like an ox; proud of his strength, and arrogant because he had a reputation that made all men wary of approaching him. He walked with a swagger, his heavily muscled shoulders straining his red shirt. His face was fleshy, and round like a full moon; his dark eyes hog-like, thick lips twisted into a sneer as he stepped on to the porch. He was wearing range clothes, although he had never chased a steer. Two gunbelts were buckled around his thick waist, each with a tied-down holster containing a .45 pistol.

'If you ain't happy with the way I run things around here then gimme my time and I'll slope,' said Morgan, his keen gaze on Logan. 'I do the work of two men around here and you're still not satisfied. I can get twice the pay you give me for half the work down Sonora way, so quit your bellyaching, Harlan.' His right hand eased towards his flared gun butt and he transferred his attention to Logan.

'Who are you, punk?'

Don't stand there asking questions,' Harland rapped. 'Do your job. Get rid of him, and if he won't go quietly then take care of him.' Harlan turned to re-enter the house, but Logan's sharp voice halted him and he swung around.

'Just hold it a minute, Harlan, and I'll tell you my business,' said Logan sharply.

'Do you reckon I'll be interested? Do your job, Morgan.'

Morgan's lips took on a vicious twist and he reached for his right-hand gun. Logan, anticipating the move, set his gun hand into motion. His pistol came fast and easily into his hand and the sound of it being cocked induced hesitation in Morgan's draw as the muzzle of his pistol cleared leather. An involuntary shiver ran along his spine but he continued his draw. Logan's gun blasted and gun-smoke flared. Morgan jerked and spun halfway around as the .45 slug slammed into his right shoulder. He dropped his gun, folded at the waist, and fell to the porch. Harlan gasped, was frozen in his doorway, his hand easing away from his waist, his stomach muscles tensed in anticipation of a slug coming his way.

'Who are you and what do you want?' Harlan demanded.

'I'm a Texas Ranger.' Logan's tone did not change. 'I'm in the county because there's trouble around here.' He glanced towards the gate and saw the guard staring in their direction.

The guard raised his rifle to his shoulder and squinted along the sights. Logan fired without seeming to aim and, although it was a long shot for a pistol, the guard dropped his rifle and fell over backwards in the dust.

'Like I said, I'm a Ranger, and I'm here because of trouble.' He explained the incident involving Mrs Shadde. 'I had to kill the four men involved, and now I'm looking for the cow spread that employed them. Are any of your crew missing?'

Harlan shook his head. 'Whoever the four are, they don't ride for me. Why didn't you say first off who you are? I'm a law-abiding man, and you won't get any trouble from my brand. I'll help the law whenever I can — just ask the local sheriff. We are loaded for trouble, and there has been some on the range, but I guess Tented H is too big for the badmen to handle.'

'I want you to ride into town and take a look at the four men I killed. I need to get them identified.'

'I was planning on riding into town today anyway,' Harlan mused. 'I'll look up the sheriff and do what I can to help. Will that satisfy you?'

'Sure thing! Now you'd better take a look at your men — I tried not to kill them. When I ride out, Morgan will be under arrest for trying to shoot me.' Logan paused, looked Harlan in the eyes, his gaze intent, and said, 'I'm not forgetting that you ordered him to shoot me but I'll reserve my decision about you until I know more about the trouble. Tell me about any problems you've had around here.'

'Like I said, I reckon we're too big to be bothered,' Harlan shrugged. 'I've heard about night-riders bothering folks on the range, and there's been some rustling. Apart from that there's nothing to talk about.'

'That's not how some people are seeing the situation,' Logan said. 'Cole Shadde was shot down on his spread this morning, and the four hardcases I mentioned were chasing Mrs Shadde with the intention of shooting her. If I hadn't been on hand Mrs Shadde would be dead now.'

'I've never heard of anyone being killed.' Harlan went to Morgan's side and dropped to one knee to check the gunman's condition. 'You hit him in the shoulder. He'll live. I'll take him into town if you like and let the doc look at him before handing him over to the sheriff.'

'I'll trust you to do just that.' Logan nodded. 'I'm riding on to the Wadham spread now. Give me directions for reaching there.'

He listened to Harlan's terse voice and then turned his horse to leave, but paused and fixed Harlan with a keen gaze.

'I don't know if you're a man who takes chances so toss your gun out across the yard before I turn my back on you, and do the same with Morgan's pistols.'

Harlan shook his head but did as he was told, and Logan set off across the yard. He paused beside the guard, lying prone in the dust, and noted that his shot had struck the man in the shoulder. He glanced back once and saw Harlan standing motionless beside Morgan. In the background he saw several men, attracted by the shooting, emerging from the bunk house and hurrying toward the house.

Facing the trail, Logan fancied that he had not wasted his time visiting Harlan. He had much to consider about the set-up at Tented H, and sensed that his duties would bring him up against Harlan again in the near future. He headed for Circle SW, following the directions he had been given, and had barely travelled a mile when he heard the sound of hoofs pounding to his rear. He glanced over his shoulder and saw three riders galloping after him. Gunsmoke blossomed around the trio as they drew within range, and Logan set spurs to his mount and hit a gallop as the crash of shooting shattered the brooding silence. Flying lead zipped past his head and whined around him.

So much for Harlan being a law-abiding man, Logan thought as he headed over a ridge and settled himself lower in his saddle. He assumed that the Tented H rancher had sent some of his gun-hands to kill him, knowing that he was a Texas Ranger, and for the moment he was content. He needed some action to bring the badmen out of their cover, and this was the only way he could do it . . .

3

Logan soon discovered that his mount was faster than those horses pursuing him, and he kept out of range of the pistol shots that came his way in the first mile of the chase. He maintained his direction to the SW ranch as he considered what he should do about the trio on his tail. He needed one prisoner at least in order to gain information, and decided that he had to set a gun trap to end the pursuit. When he topped a ridge that dropped him out of sight of the trio, he drew his Winchester from its saddle-boot and got down from his mount to crawl into a firing position on the ridge.

The three riders were ascending the slope, riding straight into the muzzle of his long gun. Logan jacked a cartridge into the breech and sighted the weapon at the foremost of the riders. He had no from cover for they had attacked him without warning, and their shots had been intended to kill.

He cuffed sweat out of his eyes and drew a bead on his target; he squeezed the trigger. The crash of the shot whipped across the range, but he hardly heard it. He saw the foremost rider pitch sideways out of his saddle. The remaining two swung away immediately, one heading to the right and the other moving in the opposite direction, seeking cover. Logan aimed at the nearest and fired again. Gunsmoke flared and echoes fled to the horizon. His target fell from his saddle and remained motionless.

Logan aimed at the last rider's horse and, when he fired, the animal cartwheeled on the slope and then sprawled lifelessly. The rider hit the ground and relaxed. Logan got to his feet, remounted his horse, and rode back down the slope to check the results of his shooting.

He discovered that the man he intended to take prisoner was dead — neck broken in the fall from his horse. The first man he had shot was lying on his back. There was blood on his upper chest, but he was still alive, breathing heavily through his gaping mouth. The third man was dead. The two surviving horses were on their feet — one was grazing on the lower slope.

Logan searched all three bodies and collected the odds and ends he found on them. He studied the inert faces, wondering who they were and why they had attacked him. The wounded man had taken Logan's slug in the chest, and was bleeding heavily. His eyes flickered open when Logan touched him. He groaned and tried to get up but Logan pushed him down.

'Stay still while I fix your wound, feller,' Logan advised him, and the man relaxed with a groan. He was wearing a beard, was around thirty years old, and was dressed in stained range clothes. His empty pistol holster was tied down were smooth and unblemished, and ruled out the possibility of a career in nursing cows. His face, now set in hard lines of pain, was twisted, his lips compressed. He had all the signs of a hardcase stamped on his taut features.

Because of the nature of his job, Logan always carried some bandaging in a saddle-bag. He fetched it and treated the man's wound, plugging the bullet hole with a screw of cloth and putting a linen pad over it. Then he sat back on his heels and surveyed his stony-eyed prisoner.

'It's time to talk,' he said. 'What's your name? How come you and those other two were shooting at me?'

'We figured to rob you.'

'So you're common thieves. What's your handle?'

'Buck Thompson.'

'Have you got a job somewhere around here?'

'I ain't worked regular since I was eighteen years old.'

'You hire out your gun?'

'I didn't say that.'

'Don't try and get smart with me. Just answer my questions truthfully.'

'You sound like you're a lawman.'

'I'm a Texas Ranger.'

'The hell you say! So we picked on the wrong man. Just our luck! Where are my two sidekicks?'

'They're both dead. If you don't work on this range then tell me where you're from.'

'We were just passing through, riding the chuck line, and were making for the big ranch back yonder for a handout. We saw you leave and thought it was a good idea to hold you up and relieve you of your dough.'

'That turned out to be a bad idea. I'm gonna take you to Alder Creek and stick you in the calaboose until I can find out more about you. Come on, up on your feet and I'll put you back on your horse.'

Logan helped Thompson up and, when they turned to where the two up in the brush some ten yards away. It was a girl, and she was holding a twelve-gauge double-barrelled shotgun in her hands. The weapon moved slowly to cover Logan, and as he looked into the twin barrels a shiver of some intangible emotion ran up his spine.

'What's going on here?' The girl's face was taut and her blue eyes were narrowed, filled with suspicion.

Logan studied her for a moment. He was supporting Thompson with both hands and his pistol was in its holster. His rifle lay upon the ground beside the spot where Thompson had been stretched out. The girl was in her middle twenties, Logan judged, and she was one of the most beautiful females he had ever seen. She was wearing a leather divided skirt, which was fringed around the bottom hem, and a leather vest, with fringes around the breast pockets and from cuffs to shoulders. Her riding boots reached halfway up her slender calves and she wore a flat-crowned Stetson pushed back from her forehead, revealing blonde hair. Although she was frowning and tense, her face was the most refreshing sight Logan had seen in a long time. She exuded beauty. Every plane of countenance enhanced her appearance, and Logan could only stand, supporting Thompson, gazing at her.

'Well,' she demanded, 'what is going on here? I heard the shooting from the other side of the ridge. What happened? Those two men over there are dead, and Denton is hurt pretty badly, by the look of him. You must have done the shooting! Are you a badman?'

'Who is Denton?' Logan asked.

'You're holding him up. Why did you shoot him?'

'He told me his name is Thompson. Do you know him, ma'am?'

'I'm Loretta Wadham; *Miss* Loretta Wadham. My father, Sam Wadham, owns the SW ranch, which is a couple of miles south of here. The man you're supporting is Frank Denton. He's on

51

you've killed. They are Bussey and Tipple, and they are supposed to be riding the north line, so what are they doing around here? And why did you shoot them?

'One question at a time,' Logan said, 'and please point that shotgun some-place else, Miss. I was on my way to see Sam Wadham at Circle S when these three attacked me. I had to shoot them in self-defence.'

'Why do you want to see my father? Are you planning to shoot him? Who are you? Do you ride for Tented H? You look like the type of man Harlan takes on his payroll.'

'I'm a Texas Ranger, Miss. I'm in the county because of the trouble around here. Can we continue this conversation at your ranch? Denton, as we'd better call him, is bleeding badly, and needs better attention than I can give him.'

'Can you identify yourself?' The twin muzzles of the shotgun continued to stare into Logan's face, and he could see that her finger was tense on the trigger.

Logan eased Denton around until the wounded man's weight was resting on his left hip and then reached into his right vest pocket and produced his Ranger law badge; a small silver star set inside a silver circle. It gleamed in the sunlight as he showed it to her, and she came forward and gazed at it intently.

'How do I know that's genuine?' she demanded.

'You'll have to take my word for it.' Logan returned the badge to his pocket. 'Let's get on to your father's ranch, shall we? You can put away your shotgun; it's scaring the hell outa me.'

She lowered the weapon but watched him closely as he took Denton to where two horses were standing. Logan heaved the groaning man into the saddle of one horse and then led the animal up the slope to where his own mount was waiting. The girl followed him, and he was aware that she remained out of arm's length gun tightly as if expecting him to turn suddenly on her.

'Where's your horse, Miss?' he asked as he swung into his saddle.

'It's along there, in cover,' she replied, pointing to the right with her gun, and she began to walk in the direction she had indicated.

Logan followed her, leading Denton's horse, and told her about the attack on Cole and Dinah Shadde at their ranch earlier.

'I had to kill the four to save Mrs Shadde's life, and I'm wondering if there are any more of your crew absent from their place of work.'

'What kind of a ranch do you think my father operates?' she demanded.

'Three of your men attacked me,' he reminded her.

'Then come along and talk to my father.' She walked on at a faster pace, and then slowed and looked up at him. 'What happened to Cole Shadde?' she asked.

'He was shot. We took him into town to see the doctor. I think he'll live.'

'Oh, poor Dinah! Where is she now?'

'I left her in town.'

'I'll go to her. We're good friends, and I can imagine how she's feeling right now.' When they reached the spot where her horse was standing, she put her gun in a scabbard and then swung lithely into the saddle. She looked into Logan's face as she heeled the animal into motion. 'Follow me and I'll lead you into the ranch. My father will be shocked by your news and by what has happened to you. We have some pretty tough men riding for us, but I don't think they are capable of doing what you describe.'

They followed the line of the ridge for a couple of miles, descended to the range, and presently came in sight of a cattle ranch in a valley that opened up before them. A man was standing on the porch of the house, watching them intently as they rode across the hard pan of the yard.

said Loretta with a tinge of pride in her voice.

Logan, who had been considering the salient points of the incidents that had ensued, was still uncertain about what was really happening. In his experience, there were always wheels within wheels in this type of situation, and he was never impatient to place suspicion. He needed proof, and although he was doubtful about Tented H, its owner, and his crew, he was loath to set his mind in their direction until he had checked them out completely.

He turned his thoughts back to what was going on and studied the man standing on the porch as they drew up in front of the house. Sam Wadham was solid-looking, had a wide forehead topped with black hair that showed a great deal of grey. He lounged in his doorway, almost filling it completely, and his smoke-grey eyes were fixed steadily in an hard gaze at Logan, who returned the stare with interest. He saw that Wadham was dressed in range clothes, which seemed to be of expensive make and made to measure, for he filled every inch of them.

Wadham smiled indulgently as he greeted his daughter, revealing strong white teeth. His features bore the marks of a long, outdoor life. When he spoke his voice had a rough quality, but was not ill-humoured. 'Gosh, Loretta, when you said you were going out hunting for the pot I expected you to bring home an antelope at best, but what have you got here? One of them is Denton, I can see, and he's been plugged. But who is the stranger?'

Logan sat his mount quietly while Loretta Wadham launched into a narration of what she had encountered on the range. While she spoke, her father nodded from time to time but did not interrupt her explanation; his keen gaze was fixed unerringly on Logan. When the girl fell silent, Wadham advanced on Logan, his hand outstretched.

in the Rangers,' he said, 'but this is the first chance I've had of meeting one in the flesh.' They shook hands. 'Get down and come into the house,' he continued. 'So Denton and his two saddle pards attacked you without warning, huh? I sure wanta hear Denton's account of what happened, and why they were not riding the north line like they were ordered to.'

Logan stepped down from his saddle. He eased Denton off his horse. Wadham stepped to the edge of the porch and shouted across to the corral, where several figures were milling around.

'Milton, come over here with a couple of the men. Denton's been shot, and I want you to take care of him.' He waited until three figures started across to the house, and then turned to the watchful Logan. 'Milton will patch him up and he'll be ready to ride to town with you when you leave. But first I want Denton to talk to me. Bring him inside.'

Logan helped Denton into the ranch house. The wounded man was semi-conscious and leaned heavily on Logan's arm. When he was eased into a chair he lolled as if about to lose his senses completely. Wadham grasped him impatiently and shook his left shoulder.

'Come on, Denton,' he rapped. 'You ain't that badly hurt. You're gonna talk to me before you leave here. I wanta know what's going on. There's a lot of trouble on this range and I've managed to keep clear of it so far. I won't have any of my crew getting involved. Open your eyes and tell me why you were not riding the north line like you were told.'

Denton's eyes flickered open and he looked around. His face was pale; he was still losing blood. There was a defiant expression on his face and he shook his head slightly before closing his eyes.

'I'll get him to talk when he's behind bars,' Logan said. 'But there's a killed four men who were attacking the Shadde ranch earlier this morning. They had shot Cole Shadde and were chasing Mrs Cole; shooting at her. Are any more of your outfit missing today? I have a sneaking feeling the attackers weren't just riding by. I reckon they work locally.'

'Do you figure those saddletramps came from here?' Wadham was horrified and it showed in his face and grey eyes. 'Hell, no!' he exploded. 'Ain't it bad enough that three of my men slouched off this morning and got the hell shot out of them? I ain't missing any more of my crew, and I'll keep my eyes peeled in future.'

'Leave Denton,' Logan said. 'I'll get him to town. Tell me what trouble you've had recently.'

'I lost some cows a month ago. Followed 'em for ten miles and then lost their trail in some bad country north of here. It was as if they sprouted wings and flew off the range. There

60

have been night-riders around, shouting and shooting off their guns, but we couldn't catch them — didn't even set eyes on them.'

'Have you got any idea who's back of it?'

Wadham shook his head slowly. 'If I had any idea I'd look them up and teach them a lesson they'd never forget. There's nothing but talk on this range. You can hear the chins wagging in town. Everyone talks, but when it comes down to it they don't know a damn thing. Even the law can't answer any questions. I've seen Deacon riding out, doing the rounds. He drops in here regularly to check with me, but he doesn't know what's going on. But take it from me, Logan; a lot of stock is being stolen off this range.'

'And nobody has any idea where it's going, huh?' Logan nodded. 'Well, that figures. I guess I'd better be pushing back to town. Pass the word to the sheriff in Alder Creek if you do learn anything that will help me.'

Denton in?'

Logan shook his head. 'He won't be any trouble. Give me a hand to put him back into his saddle.'

Wadham raised his gravelly voice, called for Milton, and a tall, lean cowhand appeared in the doorway. Wadham gave some orders and Denton was taken outside.

'I'm sorry I can't do more to help you, Logan,' Wadham said as they stepped out to the porch.

Logan saw Denton being roped into his saddle. He was groaning and white-faced; he was in a semi-conscious condition, and his eyes were closed. Loretta Wadham was in her saddle, her lovely face stamped with impatience.

'I'm going into town now to see Dinah Shadde,' she said. 'May I ride with you for company, Mr Logan? It's got so this range ain't safe these days for a lone woman to travel.'

Before Logan could reply a bullet struck the front of the house and window glass shattered and flew. Logan dashed to the girl's side and snatched her out of the saddle. He dropped to the ground with her as a fusillade of shots blasted out the silence. One of the two cowhands cried out and fell lifeless on the porch. Logan looked up and saw Wadham diving back inside the house. The front of the building was riddled with flying slugs; windows were smashed. Denton's horse was hit and fell squealing to the ground, its hoofs threshing wildly before it finally relaxed in death. Denton was trapped by one leg beneath it.

Logan drew his right-hand pistol, but refrained from replying to the threat. The range was too great for a handgun. He noted that gunsmoke was coming from at least six positions beyond the gate, and there was nothing he could do but lie quiescent under the gun storm and wait for it to pass.

When the shooting stopped, Logan got to his feet. He spotted at least two riders galloping away in the distance emerged from the house, holding a Winchester in his big hands.

'I'll be back,' Logan called as he raked his mount's flanks with his spurs. He galloped across the yard and set out in pursuit of the fleeing riders, his mind occupied with conflicting impressions of what was happening. He needed prisoners in order to acquaint himself with the knowledge needed to bring about a conclusion to his investigation, and as he rode hell for leather he realized that his job was barely beginning. He had a long, arduous trail to ride.

He was following two men, but he saw two more riders in the distance, and guessed that they were of the same party. He could not even guess at what was going on. He had killed four unknown gunmen who had attacked Cole Shadde and his wife, and then suffered an attack by three of Wadham's men. So where did that leave Wadham? Was he behind the trouble and covering his tracks, or was Harlan at Tented H responsible? Logan pushed on. There was only one way he could discover what was going on and that was to capture one of the guilty men and make him talk . . .

4

Logan began to close in on the two riders he was following. They were galloping to the north; he settled himself for a long ride, his eyes gleaming as he watched his quarry, who were apparently unaware of his presence. When he was in a position to make out their details he studied their horses — one animal was a big grey, the other a brown horse with a great deal of white about its legs. The two riders were range-dressed; one wore a red shirt and a yellow neckerchief, the other was more soberly dressed; set up in a grey shirt and a black bandanna. They were in no hurry now, but moved as if they had some specific destination, and Logan decided against riding them down and settled to follow them, hoping they might lead him to others who were causing local trouble.

When they hit a trail that headed north-west toward the Big Bend country, Logan stayed behind, keeping a little to one side to avoid being spotted. He reined in on a ridge and watched the two men, following their trail. He waited until they were close to a ridge, but as he started forward to continue in pursuit he saw a big freight wagon pulling along the trail ahead of the pair, driven by the freighter, Jake Larter, and escorted by a rider who was heavily armed.

The pair of riders Logan was trailing reined in beside the wagon, which halted, and the men chatted for several minutes before Logan's quarry continued on their way. The big freighter waved a cheery hand to the pair as they departed, and then whipped his team and continued on too. Larter hadn't stayed long in Alder Creek, Logan mused. He waited until they were almost abreast of him before riding into view. He descended from the ridge to meet the wagon.

came forward several yards and reined in when he was clear of the team. He was holding a Winchester across his saddle, its muzzle pointing in Logan's general direction. Logan approached, holding up his right hand, and the big freighter brought his team to a halt. Logan reined in beside the escort. The man was tall and thin, dust-covered, a hard-bitten man with a face the colour of old-leather, sun-dried and expressionless. His eyes were pale blue, filled with suspicion. The freighter, seen close up, was big, fleshy, over-weight, and in his fifties. His face was craggy. His brown eyes were filled with suspicion, and something more. His left hand rested on the butt of a shotgun that was lying on the seat at his side, and he looked ready to spring into action at the drop of a hat.

'Howdy?' Logan said. 'I saw you pull into Alder Creek earlier. Where are you heading now?'

'Who wants to know?' Larter demanded. 'I saw you back there in town. You're covering a lot of ground, huh? Do you want something from me?'

'I'm hunting two men. They are part of six riders who attacked Sam Wadham's SW spread while I was there and shot the hell out of it. They split up after leaving, and I took out after two of them. They were heading in this direction the last time I saw them.'

'Are you a lawman?' Larter demanded.

'I'm a Texas Ranger,' Logan replied. 'Have you seen two men riding this way?'

'We ain't seen a soul since leaving Alder Creek,' cut in the man on the horse.

'Who are you?' Logan demanded.

'Tom Barden. Larter and me are pards in the freighting business.' Bardon was on edge, and his long gun was pointed at Logan as if he hoped to use it. 'We're heading for Buffalo sundown.'

'Sorry if I'm holding you up.' Logan was wondering why Larter had lied about seeing the men he was following. They had obviously been well known to each other, and Larter had waved a farewell hand when the two hard-cases rode on. But Logan did not refer to it. 'I guess I better back track a spell and look for their trail,' he said. 'See you around.'

As he turned his horse to ride back the way he had come, he saw a loaded pack horse tied to the back of the wagon. He did not like his back being towards Larter and his pard, and experienced a shiver of anticipation until he drew out of range. He did not look back, but as soon as he was out of sight of the freighters he reined in and sat his saddle, watching their progress as they headed for Buffalo Crossing.

Logan knew that Larter had lied, and again wondered why. The obvious reason was that Larter did not want the two men arrested, and that knowledge opened up a fresh trail of thought for Logan. He tucked the knowledge into a corner of his mind and went on, circling away from the trail to pick it up again well ahead of the wagon. He had seen the spot where the two men he was following had disappeared, saw their fresh tracks, and continued following them; they eventually left the trail and headed west.

The nature of the terrain changed from wide open spaces to close country; it became broken and difficult to traverse. Logan looked ahead; he was following two sets of tracks and was riding into the foothills of a range of mountains purpled by distance. There were other tracks of horses around, and cattle had been pushed through recently on the same trail followed by his quarry. He was heartened by the signs and went on expectantly. He did not think the badmen would hide out too far from the range they were working over.

slumped in his saddle, his hat brim low over his eyes, but he straightened quickly and came to full alertness when a distant shot reverberated from ahead. He listened to the fading echoes, cuffing sweat from his forehead. Heat was striking burnished, copper-coloured rocks and the brilliance of the sun was almost too much to bear. He looked around as he moved on, checking skylines and approaches. Nothing was moving at ground level, but soon he saw the lazy flight of a number of buzzards wheeling in the sky, and studied them for several moments, noting their position. It seemed that they were interested in something ahead of him, and he pushed on to check, wondering about the shot he had heard.

When he emerged from a gully and encountered a rock-strewn stretch of level ground he reined in again, for a horse was down ahead of him. He kneed his horse into cover. Two men, mounted on one horse, were riding over a ridge several hundred yards to the west. Logan let them disappear from view, and then waited patiently to give them time to draw ahead. Going on, he loosened his right-hand pistol in its holster and kept his hand close to the butt. This was ambush country!

He reined in beside the dead horse. It had stepped into a hole and broken a foreleg.

The buzzards were swooping around, waiting for him to move out, and he touched spurs to his horse and went on, following the tracks in the dust. He was beginning to suffer from the heat. He had enough food and water for a couple of days, though, and a small bag of oats for the horse was strapped to his cantle.

The two men ahead were travelling slowly now, and just when Logan began wondering where they were hiding out he heard a shout echoing through the rocks. He halted and dismounted, led the horse into cover, and trailed his reins. He took his Winchester from its keeping to one side of the single line of tracks he was following.

Within moments of hearing the shout he was crouching behind a rock and looking out at the entrance to a gorge, a narrow slash in a high wall of rock. A man was standing there with a rifle in his hands, looking up at the two men on the horse. There was coarse laughter, and then the men on the horse entered the canyon, passing out of Logan's sight, and he was left to gaze at the guard, who disappeared behind a rock.

Logan went back to his horse and moved it away from the canyon entrance. He took time out to give his horse a drink from his canteen, using his hat, and doled out a couple of handfuls of oats before attending to his own needs. He swallowed a mouthful of water and then ate hard tack from his precious supplies. Afterwards he went back to the canyon entrance.

He made a slow approach to the

canyon, staying in cover and angling away from the spot where the guard had gone. He flattened out and bellied forward the last few yards, and when he could look into the gorge he saw a wide stretch of rough stones littering the passage through the ridge forming the front wall of the canyon. He smelled tobacco smoke. The breeze was coming from the west, and he located the guard sitting in the shade on a rocky ledge about ten feet above the ground, watching the approaches to the gorge from cover.

Logan could see grass inside the canyon, and he needed to get closer to check it out. He didn't doubt that the badmen were hiding here, and eased away to his right, staying in cover, slipping from rock to rock until he had passed through the entrance. When he was safely past the guard he paused and studied a totally different vista facing him. The gorge ran from north to south and its floor was covered entirely with knee-high grass. There had to be water wide stream to the north, saw three cabins and a corral, and noted that a large herd of cattle was present.

He stayed by the canyon wall and went forward cautiously — he needed to check out the herd. The ground close to the rock wall was littered with rocks and he was able to remain in cover most of the time. He drew level with the cabins and stayed low as he studied them. Several men were gathered in a group in front of the middle cabin, and some women were among them. The corral was crowded with horses. He counted more than twenty, and considered the implications of such a large group of men living out here in the wilderness.

He continued up the gorge, drew closer to the cattle, and was not surprised when he saw several different brands on the animals. Rustled stock! He recognized the Tented H brand, Sam Wadham's SW, and others he did not know. He was elated that he had discovered the hideout of the badmen he was seeking, and realized that he had to get back to town for a posse.

He began to retrace his steps, moving slowly but surely back down the canyon towards the entrance. He paused frequently, checking his surroundings, but there was not much activity around the cabins. He could hear the loud voices and raucous laughter of the badmen. They sounded as if they were having a good time, but he was determined to change all that.

He was close to the rocky entrance when he heard the sound of approaching hoofs. He slid behind a rock and drew his right-hand pistol. The guard called a challenge and a harsh voice answered.

'Hi yuh, Pete! This is Billy Parker. You'll never guess what I just picked up skulking in the rocks.'

'Do tell!' the guard replied.

'A female, and she fought like a wild cat.' Parker chuckled.

'What's she doing out here? Maybe

hanging around the camp.'

'I'll take her in and dump her on Dolan. I can't wait to see his face when he gets a look at her. And you better keep your eyes skinned, Pete. If a female is hanging around then there could be a posse out looking for her.'

'No one can get in here,' replied the guard confidently, and Logan grinned.

A woman's voice sounded, angry and indignant. Hoofs clattered on rock and Logan braced himself. Two horses appeared, passing the guard's position, and Logan felt a chill sensation in his stomach when he saw the woman: it was Loretta Wadham, and she was roped to her saddle, looking hot and bothered. Her hat hung down her back, suspended by its chin strap, and her hair was disarrayed. The man with her, Parker, was hard-faced, brutal, and there was no sympathy in him for his prisoner. He jerked on the rope wrapped around his saddle-horn, which was attached to Loretta's bridle. He was grinning harshly, as if enjoying himself with a woman in his power. His dark eyes were glinting with an unholy light.

'You'll soon open that pretty mouth of yours when Dolan gets his hands on you,' Parker declared. 'Come on.'

Logan eased sideways around the rock that was covering him. When the horses drew almost level with him they were just out of arm's length and he arose swiftly, his pistol cocked and pointing at Parker's chest.

'Keep quiet,' Logan said. He could not see the guard for his position was screened by a buttress of rock, but he knew the man could hear plainly.

Parker lifted his right hand instinctively to his holstered gun, but stopped the motion before he touched the weapon and eased his hands away from his waist.

'Get down from your horse,' Logan commanded, and he snatched a pistol from Parker's holster as the man complied. He swung the Colt and temple. Parker gasped and fell limply. Logan stepped up into the vacated saddle and wheeled the animal to face the entrance. He put a finger to his lips, cautioning silence, and Loretta nodded, white-faced. When he went forward, the girl's horse followed closely.

Logan glanced around. They seemed to be alone, except for the guard. They reached the guard's position, and saw him standing behind his cover, watching the ground outside the hideout.

'Hey, Pete,' Logan called, levelling his pistol at the man. Pete's head came round quickly, and he began to swing his rifle to cover Logan.

'Don't try it,' Logan advised. 'Throw the rifle over your cover and climb down here. Make it quick.'

Pete hurled his weapon away as if it had suddenly become too hot to handle. He jumped down from his rocky perch and stood motionless with his hands raised shoulder-high. Logan kneed his horse within reach and slammed his pistol barrel against Pete's head.

'Come on,' Logan rapped as Pete crumpled to the ground. 'Let's get moving. We need to lose ourselves before the alarm is raised. We won't have much time.'

He spurred his horse and left the canyon, followed closely by Loretta. As they drew away from the hideout, Logan heard the guard begin shouting, and then a rifle was fired, the shot echoing seven times across the wilderness. He glanced over his shoulder but they were in cover, with rocks between them and the entrance. He set a fast pace back the way he had come earlier, intent on getting Loretta back to her father's ranch.

When they were well clear they halted to rest their horses and Logan turned to Loretta.

'I got the shock of my life when I saw you coming into the canyon tied to your saddle,' he said. 'How did you get yourself into that situation?'

the spread after those men,' she replied. 'It seemed like a good idea at the time, and when I realized that it wasn't it was too late for me to turn back. I trailed you all the way, and was waiting for you to come out of that gorge when Parker appeared and forced me to go along with him.'

'You were lucky I was in a position to free you.' Logan shook his head. 'You should have known better then to get mixed up in this business. Now I've got to see you back to your spread when I need to be getting about my own business. There are around twenty badmen in that gorge, and a big herd of rustled cattle, including some SW stock.'

'We did lose some steers,' she gasped. 'I'm sorry I've caused you trouble, but I can get back home safely.'

'I can't take the risk of you falling into bad hands again,' he replied. 'Those badmen will come out of their roost like a swarm of bees, and if they get on our trail we'll be in trouble. Come on, let's ride.'

They continued, pushing their horses in the hot afternoon. Logan could feel his mount getting tired. He watched his rear continuously, and just when he thought they had succeeded in making a clean getaway he heard the sound of a shot from behind and a slug ricocheted off a rock to his right — too close for comfort. He reined into cover and Loretta joined him. She was looking scared, but drew her rifle from its saddle-boot.

'Put that away,' he told her. 'We've got to try and lose them, outrun them. Follow me closely, and keep up.'

She nodded, her mouth set in grim lines, and she stayed with him as he began to swing left and right through a cluster of rocks. More shots sounded, and echoes fled. Logan heard the smack of flying lead on the surrounding rocks; they were gaining on them. There was open range ahead, and he did not fancy his chances with no cover. He angled to and Loretta called to him almost immediately.

'Logan, there are three riders out to our left, and another two off to the right. It looks like they're aiming to cut us off.' She paused for a moment and then added: 'I can see more riders coming along behind. They're moving fast, and it looks like they'll come up with us shortly.'

'Keep riding,' he replied. 'If I were alone I'd get into cover and shoot it out with them, but I can't risk your life.'

'I'm sorry for putting you in such a dangerous position,' she replied.

'You should have thought of that before you left the ranch.' He glanced and turned his head to look at her, saw her forlorn expression, and smiled to soften his words. 'It can't be helped now so forget about it. What we've got to do is avoid being trapped.'

They continued, and Logan became aware of the three riders on their right. The trio were well mounted and inching forward all the time, almost drawing level with them, but just out of gunshot range. Logan itched to get down into cover and use his Winchester but he was handicapped by the girl's presence. He increased his pace, taking a chance because the broken ground over which they were riding was dangerous at their speed; if one of their horses put a foot in a hole or stumbled on a rock then disaster would strike.

The riders on their left were gaining all the time, easing into gunshot range. Logan drew his left-hand gun and fired at the trio. He didn't expect to hit anyone, but hoped to deter them. His second shot struck the nearest horse and the animal went down heavily, throwing its rider over its head. Logan was heartened, and increased his rate of fire. He was an exceptional shot under any condition, and soon noticed that the riders were swerving away. He hit a rider with his next shot and the man vacated his saddle.

called.

Logan looked around, his mind on their problems.

'I don't want to leave the rocks,' he said. 'If we gave them a clear shot they would be on us like a pack of wolves.'

'I know a place where we could hide up in if we could shake these men off our trail. It's in that high ground off to the left. I stumbled on it when I was helping my brother round up some strays.'

'Head for it,' said Logan without hesitation. 'Take the lead and I'll try to discourage the badmen.'

Loretta spurred her horse and went on in another direction. Logan holstered his pistol and drew his Winchester. He set his mount to follow Loretta's horse and wrapped his reins around his saddle-horn. He checked his surroundings, and then began to shoot at their pursuers. He sent a stream of well-aimed shots at the riders coming along in their rear, and stopped two men in their tracks. The remaining riders split up and kept coming. Loretta called Logan's name in a frightened tone, and he looked around to see the two men out on the right slanting in toward them. He shifted his aim, and then they hit a slope and all sight of their pursuers was temporarily lost.

They hammered over rocky ground, and Logan feared that the next step his horse took would bring disaster, but they continued. They swept over a low ridge and descended the reverse slope. The gradient was imperceptible at first, but then it dropped more rapidly, and Logan saw that they were entering a narrow gorge with bare rock walls that seemed to meet together over their heads. The sun was suddenly cut off. The air turned cold. Logan slid his rifle back into its saddle scabbard. Loretta was picking her way between the larger rocks littering the floor of the gorge. Logan pressed closer to the girl, and then his horse put a hoof into a hole, instantly.

Logan kicked his feet out of his stirrups and vacated the saddle in a sideways dive that carried him clear of his stricken mount. He hit the hard ground with an impact that drove the breath from his body and slumped for a moment, aware that this was it. With no horse he was at the end of his trail. There were badmen all around, and he could not hope to beat them all. His only chance had been to fight them in small groups, but now, when they mustered their strength they would come in with guns blazing and swamp him, and he would be afoot . . .

5

Logan staggered to his feet and bent over his horse. The stricken animal was holding up its broken foreleg, emitting grunts of pain, its eyes rolling. Logan drew his pistol and put the beast out of its misery, aware that the sound of the shot would attract their pursuers. The gunshot seemed to echo endlessly within the tall, rocky walls as he drew his rifle from its scabbard, unstrapped his saddle-bags from the cantle, and hurried after Loretta, who, having seen him regain his feet after the fall, was riding slowly along the gorge.

'It's not far now,' she said encouragingly when he reached her. 'Let's try and get under cover before those badmen spot us.'

He ran beside her horse. Sweat trickled down his face and his legs protested painfully at his exertions.

did not have enough breath to respond. She finally rode in close to the rock wall on the right, passed behind a screening clump of bushes, and rode down an uneven slope to a gaping cave mouth below the level of the floor of the gorge, in front of which ran a tiny stream of clear, cold water in a narrow gully. She reined in and dismounted as Logan caught up with her. He leaned against a rock and hunched his shoulders, trying to regain his breath while she permitted her horse to drink sparingly. Logan flopped down by the water and gulped several mouthfuls that seemed like nectar to his overheated insides.

'How'd you manage to find this place?' he demanded, looking up at her.

'I chased a steer through the bushes up there and followed it down to the cave. Come on. I've got a lantern here and a small cache of supplies. It's a long way from the spread, and I've stayed here with my brother Ben a couple of nights off and on when we've been combing for strays. We use the place to save putting up a line shack around here.'

'I met your brother Ben in Alder Creek,' he said as he got to his feet, remembering that he had not been impressed by him but saying nothing more.

Loretta led her horse into the cave. Logan followed closely, and waited in complete darkness until she struck a match and lit a candle standing on a convenient rock shelf. The cave was low, but seemed to go on forever, disappearing into the blackness beyond the candle's feeble glow.

'It's better than you think,' she said, leading her horse into the blackness. 'My brother checked all around here when we first discovered it, and found another gorge and a grassy meadow beyond it. He used dynamite to open the back of this cave, and we've kept a couple of spare horses through there ever since.'

'That will solve my immediate

should go on from here, get one of your spare horses for me, and make for your place pronto. I need to get back to town, raise a posse, and come back to that hideout for the gang.'

'I can get back home alone from here with no trouble,' she responded.

He shook his head. 'I won't hear of it. I'll see you home.'

She wouldn't argue because the sound of his tone warned her that she would be wasting her time.

'Hold on to my horse's tail. It's dark right through to the end of this cave, but it's straight and uncluttered, and it's not too far.'

Logan grasped the tail of her horse. She blew out the candle and led the animal through the darkness. After they had traversed several yards, she gave a cry, and Logan, unable to see anything, heard the sound of her falling.

'What's wrong?' he called. 'Are you okay?'

'The tunnel is blocked,' she replied.

'There's been a rock fall. 'We can't get out this way.'

'I'll go back first and check it is safe,' he said instantly. 'Those guys could have found the cave entrance by now.'

He drew his right-hand gun and started back the way they had come, his left hand outstretched, fingers running lightly over the rough face of the rock wall. Loretta followed him, the hoofs of her horse clattering on the bare rock underfoot. When Logan could see a glimmer of daylight he told her to wait and went on alone in heavy silence.

He became more cautious as the light brightened at the entrance, but the tunnel eased to the right and the light that showed was deceptive, leaving the rear of the cave in complete darkness. He halted and dropped to one knee, his gun ready for action. He listened intently but heard nothing, although his well-developed sense of danger was warning him that all was not well. When several moments had passed without incident he prepared to go on, but a

'That horse back there ain't moving now, Charlie. Go check the tunnel as far as that rock fall.'

'Why don't you go check it?' another answered.

The voices were anonymous in the darkness, and Logan could not pinpoint their positions. He took a single cartridge from a loop in his belt, flattened out on the rock floor, and tossed the cartridge into the darkness to his right. It rang metallically on a rock, and bounced a couple of times. The response was immediate. Two guns blasted a series of shots. Lances of muzzle flame split the inky blackness, and the hammering reports of the pistols sounded like thunder in the close confines of the cave.

Logan lifted his gun and fired at muzzle flame while the flying slugs struck rock and ricocheted in all directions, rebounding several times. Logan added his own grim din to the chaos, and concentrated on the two guns that were firing wildly. The noise subsided in a matter of seconds, but echoes dragged on. Logan's ears were deafened by the outburst; rang loudly in protest. He forced a yawn in an attempt to clear them, and remained motionless, although he sensed that he had hit both attackers in that short rackety hell.

A few moments later Loretta's voice called to him in a fearful tone.

'Logan, are you all right?'

He cocked his gun and waited for another outburst of flying lead as he replied.

'Sure. Stay put, and keep down. There were two of them waiting here, but I got them. I'll check them now.'

He knew by the muzzle flames of the shooting that both men had been just inside the entrance to the cave, and they would still be shooting if he hadn't hit them, but his nerves were taut and his teeth were clenched as he eased forward. His eyes had become daylight coming into the cave and he soon located both men. They were almost side by side — dead. He got to his feet and moved into the entrance, going forward slowly to check for others of the gang.

He did not leave the protection of the cave, but remained low and used his ears. He could detect no sounds, and there was no movement outside, but he could feel an urgency crowding his mind, warning him that they should get out of this trap as quickly as possible. He eased back into the cave, and called Loretta.

'Bring your horse. It looks all clear out there so we'd better get moving. Make it quick.'

He was tense and grim, but he smiled when Loretta appeared at his side, leading her horse.

'We've got to be on the move,' he said in a low tone. 'We'll have to travel slowly because this area will be teeming with badmen.'

'We've got just one horse between us,' she replied. Her face was pale and her eyes showed torment.

He took her reins, led the horse out of the cave, and paused within the screen of bushes to check the gorge.

'It looks okay,' he said.

He swung into the saddle and reached down a hand to help her mount behind him. She swung up with a lithe moment and settled behind the saddle. She slid her hands around his waist and held him tightly as he touched spurs to the mount and set the animal in motion. A sigh of relief escaped him as they left the cave behind and returned the way they had come. There was no sign of riders. The gorge was deserted.

He dismounted before they left the gorge and went forward on foot to check the terrain. When he returned to Loretta she had dismounted and was gazing up at the rim of the gorge.

'I hope I'm wrong,' she said, 'but I think I saw movement up there. It was something.'

Logan looked up and studied the skyline. He saw nothing unnatural, and turned to the horse.

'If there is someone up there he won't show himself again,' he said, swinging into the saddle. 'Come on, let's get out of here.' He held out his hand to her, and as she mounted a bullet struck the horse, which foundered immediately. The sound of the shot followed swiftly, and they both sprawled on the ground as echoes reverberated.

Logan rolled and slithered behind a rock before looking for Loretta. She was stretched out apparently lifeless. He clenched his teeth, leapt to his feet, and ran to her. He lifted her bodily and dived with her into fresh cover. There was no more shooting, and he gasped for breath as he bent to check her. Relief filled him when he discovered that she had struck her head on a rock and been knocked senseless. There was a smear of blood on her forehead but she was breathing, and he waited until she opened her eyes and looked up dazedly.

'What happened?' she demanded, putting a hand to her head.

He told her, and added to her shock by saying that her horse was dead. She sprang up and staggered to the animal; stood looking down at it in disbelief.

'We're in trouble now,' he said, shaking his head. 'It must be at least fifteen miles to your spread, and we are going to have to walk it.' He paused and grimaced. 'Unless I can go back in that robbers' roost and steal a couple of nags.'

She turned to him, her face expressing fear. 'You can't be serious,' she gasped.

'I've never been more serious in my life,' he replied. 'The only alternative is to pick up those two horses you say are in the other gorge, but I don't think I have time to do that so I'll wait until sundown and then pay a visit to Walt

'That hideout is miles away,' she said, shaking her head. 'It will take us until midnight to reach it.'

He put out his hand and touched her arm, cautioning her to silence. She looked at him with a questioning light in her eyes, until she heard the sound of approaching hoofs. Logan motioned to her to seek cover. He drew his guns and went in the direction from which the sound of horses was coming. When he stepped around a large rock he confronted two riders, and spoke in a sharp tone as he covered them with his pistols.

'Halt and throw up your hands,' he rasped.

The two men reined in quickly. Both were bearded and travel-stained. The one nearest Logan set his right hand into motion and clawed a Colt .45 out of its holster. The second man raised both his hands and sat motionless in his saddle. Logan squeezed off a shot and dust flew from the nearest man's shirt as the slug hit him in the chest. His gun fell out of his hand as he fell sideways towards his companion and vacated his saddle. He hit the ground with a thud.

Logan motioned with his left-hand gun, and the surviving stranger took his gun from its holster, using his forefinger and thumb, and dropped the weapon into the dust. He was young. His beard was thick and black. The end of his nose looked as if it had been bitten off in some long-ago fight, and the lobe of his right ear was missing.

'You're one of Dolan's gang, huh?' Logan demanded.

'Who in hell are you, riding around and shooting at men who are doing a lawful job?' the man countered.

'I'm Travis Logan, Texas Ranger. What's your name, mister?'

'Shorty Pardoe. I ride for the SW brand. Me and Pete there are combing these gorges for strays.'

Logan called Loretta and she came to his side. 'He says he's Shorty Pardoe truth?'

Loretta shook her head. 'I don't know him. He's not one of our riders.'

'You're the Wadham gal!' Pardoe grimaced. 'What are you doing out here with a Ranger?'

'Get down.' Logan said, holstering his left-hand pistol. 'We want your horse.'

Pardoe dismounted and raised his hands shoulder high. 'You ain't gonna leave me afoot out here miles from anywhere, are you?' he demanded. 'If you're a lawman like you said and I'm under arrest, then you've got a duty to take care of me.'

'Tell me about yourself and what you're doing running around with Walt Dolan,' Logan countered, 'and then I'll decide what's to be done with you.'

'I never heard of Walt Dolan.' Pardoe's mouth closed and an obstinate expression came to his face. 'Maybe I got the name of the rancher wrong. It could have been Harlan of Tented H. It was a toss-up between Harlan and Wadham for a job.'

'I can tell you're lying through your teeth, Pardoe,' Logan rasped. 'Step away from the horse and we'll be on our way. There's a cave back that way where there's some food and plenty of water. It's occupied by two of Dolan's men. They're both dead! Maybe you know them, huh? Anyway, stick around the cave and I'll send a couple of posse men out from town tomorrow and they'll bring you in.'

'What kind of a choice is that to give a man?' Pardoe demanded.

'It's the best one I've got right now.' Logan grasped Pardoe's right shoulder and pushed him into motion. 'Get moving; and you'll stay put in that cave if you've got any sense.'

Pardoe staggered away and Logan swung into the saddle of the horse the man had vacated. He motioned for Loretta to mount the second animal, and then led her the way they had to ride to reach the Wadham ranch. They

Loretta, on Logan's left, called sharply to him.

'There's a rider with a pack horse over this way,' she reported, pointing to her left.

Logan immediately reined into cover and peered in the direction she was pointing. He could see nothing.

'He's behind that wall of rock at the moment,' she said. 'He's leading a loaded horse and travelling at a walking pace. Give him five minutes and he'll be in view again.'

Logan waited stolidly, watching all approaches to their position. Two horses finally reappeared from cover and continued in a direction that would take them close to the outlaw hideout. Logan gazed at the rider, and his pulses quickened.

'He looks like Tom Barden, the partner of Jake Larter, the freighter in Alder Creek, he said. 'I saw them on the trail to Buffalo Crossing earlier; there was a pack horse tied to the back of their wagon. I wonder where Barden is heading. Have you any idea what's out this way, Loretta, apart from the hideout?'

Loretta shook her head. 'It looks like he's heading for the hideout.' Her voice shook with excitement. 'Is the freight line providing the badmen with supplies? I know there are no ranches out that way for a good thirty miles, except a horse ranch that deals in cavalry remounts.'

Logan watched Barden continuing on his lonely way. 'I guess I'll have to spend some time watching him after this,' he mused. 'Come on, let's push on. I have to get back to town. There are a number of things I need to check out.'

'Look, if you want to follow Barden then go to it. I can get home easily from here, and I'll send a man into town to tell the sheriff what's been happening out here. A posse can get here in a few hours, and you could need their help by then.'

from here,' Logan mused. 'Go on, then, and don't stop for anything. I'll call in at your place when I get through here.'

Loretta smiled and reined away. He watched her go, shaking his head as he thought of the lonely miles she had to ride. He sighed and went back to pick up Barden's trail and, dropping in behind the freighter, followed at a distance, remaining in cover. Barden was not pushing his loaded animals. Logan controlled his impatience and followed stoically.

Shadows were falling by the time Barden neared the outlaw hideout. Logan was pleased when the man reached the gorge and sang out to announce his presence. Logan saw a guard appear atop a rock, rifle in his hands.

'So it's you, Barden,' the man shouted, his voice echoing in the silent expanse of wilderness. 'Dolan's been moaning about you taking so long.

Have you got his favourite brand of whiskey?'

'I got everything he asked for and some bad news as well,' Barden replied, riding into the entrance to the gorge.

'What's the bad news?'

'There's a Texas Ranger in the county. I saw him earlier on the trail to Buffalo Crossing. He was trailing Ed Thomas and Squinty Terrell, and he came in this direction when he left us.'

'You're too late with that item,' the guard replied. 'We've had some trouble around here, and the gang rode out after a man who sneaked in and snatched a girl from one of the men who found her skulking outside the gorge.'

Logan shook his head. He moved away from the entrance and, in the gathering shadows, knee-hobbled his horse among some rocks. He gave the animal oats and then poured water into his Stetson to enable it to slake its thirst. He left the horse and went back to the hideout, Winchester in hand.

as he sneaked forward to the rocky entrance of the hideout.

Night was falling swiftly. Logan concealed himself behind a rock near the entrance and waited for full dark. He needed to scout out the hideout, identify Barden with the outlaws, catch him in a compromising situation, and then trail the freighter clear of the place and arrest him. It sounded simple, but he was tense when he finally slipped from his cover and moved through the entrance to the gorge under the nose of the guard.

Stars were bright overhead by the time he had cleared the entrance. His eyes quickly became accustomed to the night and he could see fairly well. On his earlier visit, he had imprinted the layout of the hideout in his mind, and now he moved unerringly towards the collection of huts and shacks by the stream. Silence surrounded him and nothing moved, but he was careful to change his position soundlessly, guided by yellow lamplight issuing from the buildings.

Time did not seem to exist as he closed in, excitement thudding in his chest. When he neared the buildings he heard raucous voices. Someone was strumming a guitar, and the strains of a Spanish cantina tune rang hauntingly through the shadows. There was laughter, and then a woman's voice sounded sharp and angry, followed by the crash of glass and an angry shout. Logan moved in like a preying mountain lion. He saw that one shack was set apart from the others and moved towards it, gun ready, nerves tense. There was a lighted window, but no noise emanating from it. He sneaked in close.

The night breeze coming from the upper reaches of the gorge was refreshing after the packed heat of the long day. Logan was tired, but his excitement held discomfort at bay as he prepared for action. He carried his Winchester in his left hand, stood up close to the wall of the shack, and eased lamplight was spilling out into the soft darkness.

He risked a glance through the aperture, saw Barden seated at a table with another man, and listened to their voices as they talked and drank whiskey. A woman was seated on a chair over by the door. The lantern in the shack was bright enough for Logan to get a good look at Barden's unmistakable features.

'You've got a good place here, Walt,' Barden said. He gulped a mouthful of whiskey. 'With all the comforts of home at hand, huh?'

'Why live rough when it's not necessary?' the other replied in a low-pitched voice. 'But it ain't a good life when we're on the run with a posse on our tails. Don't let the peacefulness here fool you, Tom. You stick with the freight business and sleep in a good bed every night. I'd willingly swap places with you any day.'

'You've got a great deal going at the moment. You're raking it in hand over fist. But you're taking chances now a Ranger has come on the scene. He's caused a lot of trouble since his arrival. Everyone I've met in the last couple of days is getting worried; several men have been killed. Tip Johnson of Tented H tried his luck against him and came off second best. This Ranger is hell on wheels. He's faster than most with a gun and seems to have a charmed life.'

'I reckon it was him sneaking around here earlier,' said Dolan, laughing softly.

'And you ain't worried about him? He's probably gone back to town to raise a posse. Come morning, you could be up to your neck in bad trouble.'

'We'll be long gone before he can get back here. The gang are getting ready to pull out in a couple of hours, and they're gonna gather a big herd off the range before we call it a day. When the cattle are cleared we'll hit one or two other places I've checked out and leave the county short of ready cash. I ain't worried none about a nosey Ranger.

everywhere. I reckon Rangers are badly overrated!'

'When I saw him on the trail I knew he was trouble.' Barden reached for the whiskey bottle and refilled his glass. 'I ain't gonna hang around here in case he shows up again. He's killed six men that I know about, and there could be more. I heard a lot of shooting going on as I came near to this place. The sheriff should have shot him the minute he saw him.'

Logan's eyes glinted as he listened. So Sheriff Deacon was in on the crookedness! That figured. He moved away from the window and went on to check out the other buildings, temporarily uncertain how to handle the situation. Dolan had said the gang was pulling out in a couple of hours to start a big steal. That had to be nipped in the bud. He considered his options, and decided to hit the gang where it would hurt most.

If he could set the outlaws afoot he

might be able to get a posse out from town to deal with them before they could gather their mounts. But if he rode back to town he would have to do something about the sheriff, and he needed to find out more about Deacon before relieving him of his badge and sticking him behind bars.

The other shacks housed the rest of the gang, and when Logan peered through lighted windows he could see preparations being made for a move. He left the shacks and followed his nose and ears to where the gang's horses were tied to two picket lines. There were around thirty horses, and Logan went along both lines, untying the restive animals. Before he completed the chore he heard a man's voice talking to one of the horses tied to the second line. He went forward like a shadow, pin-pointed the man's position, and struck quickly and silently.

The man fell without a sound when Logan's rifle butt crashed against his skull. The horse reared and pulled back the picket line and used a length of rope to hogtie the man. Then he freed the rest of the horses, and they began to move away, excited and nervous.

Logan lifted his rifle and fired several shots skywards. Flashes lanced from his gun muzzle and ripped through the night; heavy detonations cut through the dense silence. The horses took flight, streaming away, tightly bunched, towards the entrance. Logan went to ground and remained motionless.

The outlaws emerged from their huts. Some started shooting at shadows, and others tried to get to the horses, but the animals could not be stopped. The drumming of their hoofs marked their progress to the entrance, and then faded as they continued their flight and continued to run into open country.

Logan was satisfied that he had handed a big setback to the outlaws, although he had placed himself in their midst. They could not leave on their mounts and would still be around come sunup, and that could prove to be a big problem for one man trying to survive.

He listened to the panic sweeping through the outlaws as they gathered to discuss the situation. Someone found the hogtied man, who had regained his senses and was vociferous in relating what had happened to him. Dolan called for order and began throwing out orders.

'Some of you get after the nags,' he shouted. 'Round up what you can. The rest of you go through this place and try to get the skunk that turned them loose. I reckon there's only one man out there — that Ranger — so get him. I'll wanta gut shoot him before we leave.'

Logan stayed put while a search was made of the area around the huts. Some of the outlaws took lanterns along, and calls and shouting went on as they searched. But by degrees that hunt eased off and Logan made his way to the wall of the gorge and began to head to his horse and be ready for the gang if they moved out. He needed to keep track of them, and was grimly determined to succeed despite the odds . . .

6

Logan became aware of exhaustion as he felt his way along the rough wall of the gorge towards the entrance. He could hear men all around him; saw lanterns moving like will-o'-the-wisps in the darkness as he was hunted by the outlaws. His vision seemed to fail, and twice he fell into depressions he did not see. His rifle clattered against a rock. A gun flared somewhere close by and a slug ricocheted off a nearby rock, striking his left arm just above the elbow. He lay on the ground, winded, and closed his eyes as pain flared through his arm. A lucky shot, he thought, but not so lucky for him. He unfastened his neckerchief and wrapped it tightly around the arm.

Voices were calling through the shadows, and men converged. Logan eased in close to the rock wall, and into an overhang of rock — hanging on to his rifle desperately. He was startled by a large animal that clattered to its feet almost within touching distance and blundered away bawling like a lost calf. An outlaw yelled with laughter.

'Hey, fellers, Clancy's found the Ranger. Listen to the skunk run. It's the first lawman I heard of who is hide-bound and got a pair of horns.'

Logan breathed with relief as the search moved away from his immediate vicinity, and he watched the lanterns receding. He decided to rest and let the hunt die away. He placed his rifle close to hand, rolled on to his back, closed his eyes, and tried to sleep.

The wound kept him awake, but he drowsed despite his tenseness. Then he slipped into an uneasy slumber, and roused up just before dawn into a grey world of uncertain shadows. He was stiff in his joints and his injured arm throbbed painfully. He could not find the determination necessary to make a move. His mind seemed remote from the physical side and he could not force movement into his limbs.

He lifted his head finally, and peered around blearily. He was hungry, and could not remember the last time he'd eaten. Thirst had parched his mouth and throat. There was trembling inside him. He had to make a big mental effort to move before he broke through the inertia gripping him. His sense of routine finally exerted itself and he crawled out of the overhang and got unsteadily to his feet. Pain stabbed through his arm when he moved it and, checking it, he saw that the bullet had gouged the flesh but the bone was untouched. Dried blood encrusted the area and the flesh surrounding the wound was red and inflamed.

The early morning was heating up, the sun already peering over the rim of the gorge. He remained in cover and studied his surroundings. The first thing he noticed was that the cattle had gone from the upper reaches of the gorge, the entrance he found none, and surmised that there was a way out of the gorge to the north. He headed to the collection of shacks, looking for movement and listening for sound. He heard nothing. The gorge was like a ghost town.

He turned towards the entrance, feeling the need to get back to his horse and have a meal and slake his thirst. He checked his weapons and proceeded to walk, forcing one foot in front of the other until his body became accustomed to movement and his muscles relaxed. When he reached the narrow entrance he acted as if the guard was in his usual place and stole forward from rock to rock until he could the check the guard post was deserted.

Logan grinned as he straightened and departed from the gorge, looking for horse tracks on the hard ground. The animals he stampeded in the night had fled and were loose in the open country. He saw lots of boot tracks; liked the thought of the outlaws on foot searching for their mounts. He moved in the direction where he had left his horse, his alertness increasing, his uneasiness fading.

His horse was grazing where he had left it, and lifted its head and whinnied as he approached. His relief was overwhelming and he hurried forward to get at his supplies. His first intimation of danger came when he was opening a saddle-bag. A spurred boot behind him raked the loose shale underfoot. Logan swung around, hand dropping to his gun butt, and then he froze and raised his hands.

A man was watching him, having appeared from behind a rock, the reins of a sorrel looped around his left arm. He held a levelled Colt pistol in his right hand, a big grin on his bearded face.

'Take it easy, Ranger. I knew it was you scared that steer out of that overhang in the hideout last night;

you'd be looking for your horse this morning. And you walked right into it, didn't you? Dolan is gonna be very happy when I hand you over to him. Keep your hands up and I'll relieve you of your hardware.'

Logan felt a dull pang of despair writhe through his breast as he looked into a pair of heavy-lidded brown eyes that gleamed with amusement. The man was wire-thin and roughly dressed in range clothes that looked as if they had never been washed: stained and dusty, creased and hard-used. He dropped his reins and moved behind Logan to snatch the pistol out of his holster.

'I'm Mick Clancy. You made a fool outa me in the night and I ain't pleased about that. Where's the girl?'

'What girl?'

'There was only one girl — the one that was brought into the hideout yesterday. You snatched her and made a run for it. You better start answering my questions, Ranger, or I'll alter the shape of your face.'

'I guess you mean Loretta Wadham.' Logan had practically forgotten the girl in the events that had overtaken him. 'What do you want with her? She was heading back to her father's ranch the last time I saw her.'

'I ain't the one that wants her. Dolan reckons having her around will keep the SW outfit off our tracks.'

'I reckon snatching her will have the opposite effect,' Logan countered. 'But you can forget about her now. She's long gone.'

Clancy cursed, and the next instant Logan was rocked by a heavy blow that crashed against the back of his head. His Stetson absorbed much of the impact, but he dropped to his knees and then flattened out on hard rock.

'You reckon you're a smart feller, I guess,' said Clancy, kicking Logan in the right side. 'Get up and we'll be moving. Dolan will take care of you when we get to where we are going.

anything at all about Dolan. Think on that while we're riding, and see if you can get any comfort from it.'

Logan staggered to his feet. His head was throbbing and whirling, and he placed his hands upon his saddle and dropped his aching head against the hot leather.

'Heck, you ain't letting a little blow unseat your brain, are you?' Clancy snickered. 'Go on; get up on that horse before I really start hitting you.'

Logan found a stirrup with his left foot and hauled himself into the saddle. He closed his eyes for a moment while the world swung and tilted around him. Clancy crowded him, waving a pistol menacingly. Logan took up his reins, touched spurs to his mount, and nearly lost his balance as the animal lunged forward in response to a blow on its hindquarters from the outlaw's gun.

'Keep moving,' Clancy called. 'We've got a lot of ground to cover.'

Logan glanced over his shoulder and

saw the outlaw swinging into his saddle. Clancy caught up with him, holstering his pistol and riding just behind him, out of arm's reach.

'Head due west,' Clancy called, and Logan changed direction to comply.

They clattered through a defile and, as they emerged, half a dozen riders surrounded them with drawn pistols. Logan reined in quickly when he recognized Loretta Wadham confronting him, gun in hand. Clancy was quickly surrounded and disarmed. He cursed as he was hauled out of his saddle. Logan closed his eyes and tried to relax.

'You've been hurt,' Loretta observed. 'Get off your horse and I'll take a look at you. I'm sorry I took so long coming back but I had to talk my father into doing the right thing.'

'You turned up at the right moment,' Logan muttered, dismounting, and when his feet touched the ground his legs refused to support him and he fell on his face. Sight and sound became jumping off her horse and running to his side. He sat up and removed his hat — rubbed the sore spot on the back of his skull.

Loretta examined him, tut-tutting as she bent over him.

'What happened when I left you at the hideout?' she demanded.

'Just get me my canteen, and then find some food in my saddle-bags,' he countered. 'I can't remember the last time I ate, and I feel as if I've just crawled a thousand miles in a desert.'

Loretta hurried to his horse and returned with his canteen. Logan uncorked it and drank deeply.

'My horse needs a drink,' he said, taking off his Stetson and pouring a good measure of water into it.

Loretta took the hat and went to the horse. Logan watched the animal drink.

'There's a bag of oats behind the cantle,' he said when Loretta handed his hat back to him. 'Give him some before you attend to me.'

He sat with his eyes closed until Loretta handed him a plate containing cold beans and cheese. Logan ate hungrily.

'You're about out of food,' Loretta said. 'I have some so I'll get a fire going and make coffee. I guess we all could do with a cup right now. But let me attend to your arm first. The wound is bleeding again.'

Logan suffered her ministrations without complaint, and drank deeply when she finally handed him a cup of coffee. Ben Wadham, a big young man wearing good range clothes, blue-eyed and with yellow hair showing under his hat, came to Logan's side and stood looking down at him until Logan looked up to meet his gaze.

'I remember seeing you in town. I didn't know who you were then. I want to thank you for taking care of Loretta yesterday. She told me how you brought her out of the gang's hideout. You're real smart, Logan, and we're here to help you. Tell us what you want done caught. What shall we do with him? Do we take him to town and hand him over to Sheriff Deacon?'

'No.' said Logan hastily. 'The first thing I'll do when I ride back to town is take Deacon's law badge off him and stick him behind bars. I heard enough about him when I was in the gang's hideout to put him away for years.'

'You don't say!' Ben whistled through his teeth. 'You haven't taken long to get busy. So Deacon is involved with the badmen! I guess that's why we couldn't get him to help us when we had trouble.'

Logan got to his feet after he had finished his coffee. He felt better with food inside him. He looked around, frowning. He saw two cowboys guarding Clancy and went across to where the outlaw was sitting.

'Where's Dolan gone, Clancy?' Logan stirred the man with the toe of a boot.

'It's no good asking me.' Defiance

showed in Clancy's face. 'I'm a born liar, so my mother said. I couldn't tell the truth if I tried. You'll only be wasting your time by asking me.'

'Don't listen to his lies,' Ben Wadham said. 'There are a lot of recent tracks around here, and I've told Bob Wright to look them over. Bob can track a bird through thin air, and when he comes back he'll know where the badmen are heading, don't you worry. We'll take your prisoner to our place if you're going on to find the outlaws. Do you want anyone to ride with you?'

Logan shook his head. 'I work alone. I'll come back to your place when I've located them, and then go back to town for a posse. If we can catch the outlaws flat-footed then there's a good chance of cleaning up, and I'd like that. What you could do is get enough ranch-hands and come back to the gorge to check on the whereabouts of the stolen herd I saw in there. I saw a number of local brands there yesterday, but this morning there wasn't a single hide there, and there must be another way out'

'Did you see any SW steers?' Ben Wadham asked.

'I sure did! There was also some Tented H stock and others. Dolan and his outlaws have been stealing this range blind.'

'Okay. We'll head back to the ranch and get the whole outfit in on this. Come on, Clancy. You'll ride with us. And you're coming too, Loretta. No more trouble for you. You can leave the cattle to us, Logan.'

Loretta looked as if she would argue with her brother, but one look at Logan's harshly set face made her compress her lips and turn away.

Logan saw a rider coming towards them, and pointed him out to Ben Wadham.

'That's Bob Wright" Wadham said. 'By the way he's grinning I'd say he's found tracks heading out.'

The young cowboy came up and dismounted. He was tall and thin, his sharp face wearing a big grin.

'A big bunch headed west, Ben,' he said, hunkering down beside a small fire Loretta had lighted to make coffee. He picked up a cup and helped himself to coffee from the pot and stood up to drink it. 'I saw by some of the tracks that horses had been rounded up and gathered — there were a dozen different boot tracks among the rocks.

'The animals were driven back into the gorge, and then came out again, carrying riders, judging by the depth of the tracks. I rode a good way to see which general direction they finally went, and they kept going west at a fair lick. You know, there's nothing out that way for fifty miles. If they ain't leaving the county then I figure they'll stop over at Benton's horse ranch, which is about fifteen miles from here.'

'I'll follow their tracks,' Logan said. 'Thanks for your help.'

'You don't reckon to take on that bunch all by your lonesome, do you?' Ben Wadham asked.

couldn't win against a bunch of outlaws. I'll locate them and then get a posse to do the job properly.'

Loretta came up, leading her horse. She handed Logan a screw of paper. 'Coffee,' she said. 'You're clean out. Don't leave it too long to see the doctor about your arm. It's a nasty wound, and it could turn bad on you.'

'Thanks for what you did.' Logan smiled at her. 'I'll be calling at your place tomorrow morning, I reckon.'

Logan cleaned his coffee pot and put the remainder of his supplies away, keeping one eye on the group of riders as they headed back for the SW ranch. When they disappeared behind a ridge he mounted and rode out to trail the badmen. The morning was slipping by, and he rode at a canter with more than a dozen sets of horse tracks to follow.

He mulled over what he had overheard in the gorge outside Dolan's shack. Big trouble was coming, and he had to be ready for it. He rode alertly, aware that the badmen would watch their back trail for signs of pursuit. His left arm was painful, and he tried to keep it up across his chest, but the jolting saddle made him suffer and he gritted his teeth as he continued.

At noon he halted to rest his horse. His surroundings were bare, except for wildlife, and the silence of the wilderness pressed in about him as he sat on a rock and considered what he had to do. He had made a good start rounding up the badmen, but did not underestimate the difficulties facing him. It was in the back of his mind that he had evidence of the sheriff's crookedness, but he needed proof, and he was uncertain of what to do next.

He had to locate the gang and finish it off, but there was also the Tented H ranch and Tom Barden, the freighter, to tackle. The future looked uncertain, but he was keen to face the problems awaiting him, and rode steadily through the long, hot afternoon towards his distant destination.

ranch buildings in the distance ahead he rode at an angle towards them, intent on approaching from a different direction. He kept to cover and took his time closing in, eventually dismounting in a draw and knee hobbling his mount. The animal immediately began to graze. Logan checked his pistols and rifle, put extra shells for each weapon in his pockets, and moved closer on foot to the ranch.

The place looked deserted, but there were more than thirty horses in the two big corrals behind the ranch house. Logan hunkered down in cover where he could watch the front and one side of the house. He removed his Stetson and lay motionless in the hot sunshine, his patience inexhaustible. Within thirty minutes he saw four different men around the place: two showing briefly in the doorway of the barn; one doing a prowler guard; and the fourth saddling up a horse and riding out, heading west.

He edged out of his cover and, despite being greatly troubled by his injured arm, made it to the rear of the barn. The sun-bleached boards were badly weathered and warped in places, and he found a convenient gap between two boards and looked into the dim interior. He saw rows of saddles and gear for a great number of horses. The two men he had seen in the doorway were lounging on a pile of hay, and they had rifles close to hand.

It looked like the gang was in occupation, and they were prepared for trouble. Logan guessed they could not be surprised by a law party, and eased away from the barn to collect his thoughts.

He needed to discover, if he could, the immediate plans of the gang boss, Dolan, and, with a little thought on the subject, decided to wait around until dark and then get within hearing distance of the house and either eavesdrop or take a prisoner. There was nothing he could do alone against the remain in one place long enough to enable him to get to town, raise a posse, and come back for a showdown.

Satisfied that there was no other way of handling the situation, Logan went back to his horse and settled down to await sundown. His arm was bothering him. There was heat in the wound and the upper arm was throbbing painfully. He ate the rest of his dwindling supplies and shared what was left of the contents of his canteen with his horse.

There were several hours left to nightfall, and he settled down to wait patiently for shadows to fall. He fell asleep without realizing what was happening, and awoke with a start. Darkness had arrived; he'd slept the hours away.

He checked his surroundings quickly and found nothing to alarm him. The ranch was silent, with only yellow lamplight at some of the windows to indicate that the place was occupied. He walked into the ranch, keeping to the shadows, and almost bumped into a prowling guard. The man, just an uncertain shadow in the darkness, came around a corner of the barn as Logan rounded it from the opposite direction.

Logan, whose reflexes were faster than average, reacted before the guard knew he was there.

He was holding his pistol, and slammed it solidly against the man's head. He heard a groan, and the clatter of a rifle hitting the ground. The man followed the long gun down, and Logan dropped to his knees, reaching out to check the man was unconscious. The guard was out completely. Logan dragged him around the corner and left him lying there. He crossed the back yard and felt his way along the rear wall of the house through black shadows that were barely relieved by lamplight shining out through the kitchen window.

As he passed the kitchen door it swung open and a big, bearded man

Logan, who was illuminated by the shaft of lamplight, for long moments. Logan steeled himself for action, but the man grinned and said:

'Have you caught anyone prowling around?'

'It's too dark to see far,' Logan replied. 'I use my ears in the shadows, and I ain't heard anything suspicious yet.'

'I'm about to make some coffee,' the man said. 'Would you like a cup?'

'Thanks. I'll give you ten minutes and then make my way back this way. I never say no to a cup of coffee.'

'I'll leave the door unlocked. Just walk in when you come back.'

Logan moved on, unable to believe his luck. His heartbeat had quickened, and he grinned with relief as he rounded a rear corner and made his way alongside the house to a front corner. Shafts of yellow brilliance from two large front windows cut through the blackness. Logan screwed his eyes half closed and flattened himself against the rough woodwork of the front wall. He was motionless for some moments, waiting for his eyesight to become accustomed to the glare, when he heard the sound of hoofs approaching the ranch.

He had no time to ease back around the front corner so he remained motionless, gripping his long gun, his breathing ragged from tension. Two riders emerged from the blackness across the yard and came to the porch. Logan did not take his eyes from them, and, as they dismounted and wrapped their reins around a hitching pole he recognized the nearer of the two men as he looked around to check his surroundings. It was Sheriff Deacon . . .

7

Logan gazed at the sheriff, wondering if Fate had delivered the lawman into his hands. The law star on Deacon's vest glinted in the lamplight. The second man was wearing a star also, but did not dismount. Instead he sat his horse, looking around as Deacon stepped on to the porch and crossed to the door of the house. Deacon hammered on the door and, when it opened, a great swathe of lamplight swept out across the yard. Logan turned his head away, wanting to retain his night vision. He dared not move, and heard a startled exclamation from the man who opened the door.

'What the hell are you doing this long way from town, Deacon?'

'I ain't happy having to ride halfway across the county just to give you a warning, Dolan. Ain't you gonna ask me in? Me and my deputy are plumb bushed. We've been in the saddle too long, and it's been a real hot day.'

'So what's your problem?' Dolan demanded. 'It must be serious to bring you out of town.'

'You don't sound worried none,' Deacon growled. 'We could do with a bite to eat.'

'Come on in then.' Dolan sounded as if he did not like the sheriff.

Logan was taking shallow breaths through his mouth. He felt like a rat caught unawares in the open, but dared not move. He heard the sheriff call to his deputy:

'Come on in, Foster. We'll eat before we start the ride back to town.'

There was the thump of boots on the ground as the deputy dismounted. 'Heck, I ain't gonna ride back to town tonight,' grumbled the man. 'My horse is plumb bushed. He needs a night's rest even if you don't. What's the damn hurry about rushing back to town? We've only just got here.'

yapping,' Dolan cut in. 'What've you got to warn me about, Deacon? It can't be that important if you're gonna stand at the door arguing with Foster. Come on in, get some grub, gimme your warning, and then get the hell back to town.'

Deacon grumbled, but his voice faded as he entered the house. The deputy followed him and the door was slammed.

Logan relaxed and moved back around the comparative safety of the corner. He was sweating, and pain flared in his left arm as he struck his shoulder against the corner of the house. He looked around, but could see nothing in the encroaching gloom. He peered around the corner along the front of the house and shook his head. The light reflecting from the windows gave him a range of vision that seemed almost as bright as day. He shook his head doubtfully as he gauged his chances. He wanted to get close to a window and listen for conversation inside the house, but if a guard appeared he could be shot down without warning.

He decided to withdraw. The guard he had rendered unconscious would soon be back on his feet, and he knew he had to be in real cover before an alarm was raised. He walked away from the house, moving slowly, and headed back to the spot where he had left his horse, aware that it would be safer to wait for Sheriff Deacon to ride back to town and get information from him there.

His horse whickered softly as he approached the animal. Away from the ranch the darkness was relieved slightly by the appearance of a half-moon peering from behind the shoulder of a distant mountain, spreading silver light through the shadows. Logan was thankful to be clear of the ranch, and prepared his horse for travel. He swung into his saddle and, as he turned the animal to get into a position from called to him from somewhere behind his left shoulder.

'Hold it right there, bucko. I've got a bead on you, and I can see you real plain. Get off the horse and throw up your hands.'

Logan hesitated for a moment, but he was caught cold. He stepped down from his saddle; lifted his hands shoulder high. Someone stepped in close to him, jabbed the muzzle of a pistol against his spine, and his guns were snatched from their holsters in quick succession and tossed into the shadows.

'You came away from the ranch, but you ain't one of the gang. Are you that Texas Ranger giving us all the trouble?'

'I'm a cowhand from Tented H,' Logan said instantly. 'I've got a message for Dolan from Harlan, who told me the gang was in the gorge, and if not they'd be here.'

'So what are you doing sneaking

around instead of riding in? Don't you know better? You're asking to be shot. Get back in your saddle and we'll ride into the ranch and you can talk to Dolan. If you ain't what you say you are then your trail will end pronto. Climb up into leather and get moving.'

Logan remounted and shook his reins. His bluff gave him a respite but he did not count too much on it. He heard hoofs behind him but did not look round as he headed back to the ranch. His thoughts were bleak when they entered the ranch yard, and he grimaced when he saw the door of the house was open and three men were standing in the shaft of light emanating from the doorway. He reined up in front of the porch, half-blinded by the glare.

'Who in hell are you?' Dolan rasped.

'I caught him sneaking back to his horse,' said Logan's captor, riding in beside Logan. 'He came from this direction so I invited him to come and talk to you. He reckons he's from

145

Harlan.'

'The hell he is,' said Deacon roughly. 'This is the Texas Ranger I've been telling you about, Dolan.'

'He is, huh?' Dolan snarled. 'Bring him into the house, Jennings. He's caused us a load of trouble. We had to leave the gorge because of him.'

'You heard the man,' said Jennings, prodding Logan with his levelled Colt. 'Get down and join the party. I wouldn't wanta be in your boots, Ranger.'

Logan stepped down. He felt unbalanced without the two pistols in his holsters. Jennings joined him, gun menacing. He lifted the Colt and struck Logan across the left upper arm; fresh agony erupted in his wound. He caught his right toe against the top edge of the porch as he lifted his foot to mount it, and pitched forward off balance. The porch came up and smacked him in the face. The glaring lamplight blanked out, and he seemed to be sliding down the side of the mountain, until total darkness and silence enveloped him.

A remote impression of searing pain flashing through the back of his head informed him that Jennings had hit him across the skull with the barrel of a pistol.

Cold sweat broke out on Logan when he returned to his senses. Brightness was in his eyes again. Harsh voices sounded over-loud in his ears, and he opened his eyes reluctantly and saw that he had been dragged inside the ranch house. Sheriff Deacon was bending over him, slapping his face with a heavy hand and calling him every bad name he had ever learned.

'Leave him to me,' Dolan rasped. 'I've got a big score to settle with him.'

Deacon grasped Logan's shoulders and dragged him upright, steadied him with callous hands that started fresh pain through Logan's injured arm. Logan brought up his right knee and it thudded into Deacon's groin. The sheriff fell away with a shout of pain.

struck out again with his pistol, and Logan went head first into the same pit of misery that had claimed him before.

This time he clung to a corner of his consciousness and prevented a long slide into the blank fog with which he was becoming familiar. His senses were unbalanced, and for several moments he did not know if he was staring at the floor or looking up at the ceiling. Rough hands grabbed at him; lifted him to his feet. A heavy fist struck his unguarded stomach — several heavy blows that made him retch. His muscles convulsed. He tried to push himself upright but his limbs refused to obey. He lay looking at a pair of legs in front of him, saw the pointed toe of a riding boot swing forward, and felt pain somewhere in his ribs.

Booted feet thudded on the floorboards and the sound of spurs tinkled musically. He saw the rowels in the end of the spurs spinning, and knew he had to get up off the floor or take more punishment than he could absorb. He rolled on to his right side and staggered into an upright position; stood swaying like a stricken tree resisting the force of a cyclone.

Deacon came at him again, but Dolan pushed the sheriff away.

'Leave him to me,' the gang boss snarled. 'Put your gun away, Jennings. I want him to talk before I kill him. I need to find out what he's learned about us. How did he come upon the gorge, and get inside it past the guard? If someone hasn't been doing his job properly then there's gonna be hell to pay. There's no room in my business for anyone who slacks off and puts the rest of us in danger.'

Logan lurched to a seat and dropped heavily into it. He looked at the men confronting him and was reminded of a pack of ravenous wolves intent on using him to relieve their hunger.

He heard Dolan's voice asking questions but could make no sense of the words. His senses were spinning ears. When he did not reply, Dolan came forward a pace and his big fist smacked between Logan's eyes. Logan tried to roll with the punch, and fell off the chair. Dolan's boot flashed in and delivered another painful kick. Again Logan dragged himself up from the floor.

The sequence continued until Dolan's impatience flared. He delivered a final kick and turned away.

'Take him out of here, Jennings,' Dolan said, biting off his words as if they burned his lips. 'Make him dig a grave behind the small barn. When he's done that, kill him silently and bury him in the hole.'

'Sure thing, boss.' Jennings drew his gun and covered Logan. 'Come on, bucko, I told you you're all washed up. Let's make this quick. I wanta get some shuteye before sunup.'

'I got a better idea,' Deacon said. 'I'll take him when we ride and drop him into a sink hole just outside of town.

It's just the place. We've dumped a lot of men in there over the years.'

'Okay,' Dolan said without hesitation. 'You should have done that with him the minute he showed up in town. It would have saved the gang a lot of trouble and extra work.

'Get your grub and then haul your freight. We'll be here a week at least, and then we're pulling out for good. Get your side of our business settled before we're ready to up stakes, Deacon, or I'll use your sink hole myself, and you know who'll be the first one to go in it.'

'Foster, put your handcuffs on Logan,' Deacon said. 'I don't want him trying anything before we get back to town.'

Logan was cuffed with his hands behind his back. He complained about his injured arm but the plea was ignored. He was thrust to the floor in a corner while the two lawmen sat down at a table and ate a good meal placed before them by the woman Logan had gorge.

'Shall I give your prisoner some grub?' the woman demanded.

'Don't bother,' replied Deacon callously. 'He'll be dead when we reach town.'

Logan lay on his right side, pain-wracked and sore. By degrees his discomfort eased until he was able to think constructively, but he did not give himself any chance of getting the better of Deacon. Apparently, the experienced lawman had been leading a double life for years: outwardly, a diligent, honest county sheriff while secretly he had been following his own crooked trail.

It was more than an hour later before Deacon arose from the table and declared that he was ready to make the trip back to town. Logan was dragged up, led outside, and thrust into his saddle. Logan relaxed when they left the horse ranch, despite the predicament he was in. But the odds against him had lessened now and he began to think of ways and means of getting the better of his two crooked captors.

They rode silently through the night. Deacon knew the area and led them unerringly through the shadows. Logan sat slumped in his saddle. There wasn't a part of his body that did not protest against his condition. His jaw was sore, there were throbbing pains in his skull, and his eyes were half-closed by blood that had congealed on his eyelids. The hours slipped by in silent agony. He drowsed in the saddle, and several times came back to full alertness just in time to prevent a fall.

The blackness of the long night gave way imperceptibly to the dull grey of dawn. When the sun lightened the eastern horizon and began to pierce the shadows, Deacon called a halt and made camp to boil water for coffee. He and Foster sat around a small fire, leaving Logan huddled on the ground nearby. Both lawmen drank coffee and, after smoking a cigarette, broke camp without giving any to Logan. They out once more, heading into the growing daylight.

There was a diversion when a great herd of cattle loomed up ahead and riders appeared, driving the steers to the west. Logan's spirits soared, thinking the herd belonged to a local rancher and he might get help. But one of the drovers came over and chatted with Deacon, calling the sheriff by name and mentioning Dolan.

Logan realized the herd was stolen; the one he had seen grazing in the gorge.

The herd passed, and Deacon sat watching it until it had gone out of sight beyond a rise in the ground.

'That's a whole mountain of dough on the hoof,' said Foster thoughtfully. 'Do we get a share of that, Sheriff?'

'You bet we do,' replied Deacon enthusiastically. 'Come on, rattle your hocks. Let's push on for town. I don't want Logan to suffer more than he has to.'

Logan looked around, his sight uneven. Both eyebrows were swollen and distorted his vision. He thought he spotted movement ahead, but when he blinked and looked again he saw nothing. Deacon moved into the lead and Foster rode in beside Logan. As they passed a draw a harsh voice called out:

'Halt and put up your hands, Deacon. We've got you covered.'

There was movement in the mouth of the draw, and three riders materialized, holding guns. Logan's heart leapt when he recognized Ben Wadham and a couple of his outfit whom he had seen earlier. Deacon halted as if he had ridden into the side of a mountain and his hands shot skywards.

'Where in hell did you come from, Wadham?' Deacon gasped. 'You gave me a helluva scare. What are you up to, sneaking around?'

'We're trailing the stolen herd that just passed you, Sheriff,' Wadham replied. 'There ain't enough of us to next best thing — trailing them. I reckoned to find out where they are going before coming to town for a posse. Who is your prisoner?'

'He's just a hardcase we picked up,' Deacon said, grinning and lowering his hands.

'Keep your hands up,' Wadham rasped. 'You're a lying skunk. Your prisoner is Logan, the Texas Ranger. Why is he in irons?'

'I'm real glad to see you, Ben,' Logan cut in. 'Deacon is working with the outlaws and he got the better of me. The deputy has the key to the irons I'm wearing, and I'd be mighty obliged if you'll turn me loose.'

Deacon's smile faded. He started to reach for his holstered gun, but Wadham's harsh voice stopped him.

'I never shot a sheriff before,' he said, 'but there's always a first time. Keep your hands up until we've drawn your teeth, Deacon. Joe, Billy, take their guns and get the key to the cuffs off Foster.'

Logan watched the two cowhands disarm the lawmen, and one of them took the handcuffs key from Foster and came to Logan's side, grinning as he removed the cuffs.

'Put them on Deacon,' Logan said.

Wadham reined in beside Logan. Daylight was strengthening.

'You look like you've been through the mill,' Wadham said.

Logan nodded. 'The information I got was worth it,' he replied. 'I'll head for town fast, get a posse out, and come back to you. I'll track the herd from here to where it's going.'

'And you'll find us somewhere behind it,' Wadham said. 'We'll be looking for you.'

Logan took the guns discarded by Deacon and Foster and stuck them in his holsters. Deacon looked disconsolate, his fleshy face displaying anxiety.

'Ride ahead of me and make for town,' Logan said. 'I'll be a couple of yards behind you. Don't try any tricks because I'm in the mood for shooting.'

tired and strained. But he was relieved by the change of circumstance, remaining alert as the hot, rough miles slipped away behind them. The day passed seemingly slowly, and the sun was well over in the western half of the sky before Alder Creek appeared on the skyline.

The town was just coming alive when they entered Main Street. Logan drew a gun and covered his prisoners as they halted outside the jail. He dismounted quickly and trailed his reins. Deacon slid out of his saddle, his expression conveying his thoughts. He opened the office door, hurried inside, and Foster followed him quickly, as if they were shy of being seen as prisoners. Logan entered and closed the door, his pistol steady in his hand.

A small man wearing a brown town suit was seated at the desk. He sprang up at their entrance, smiling a greeting, his dark eyes gleaming.

'Nothing to report, Sheriff,' he said,

and then noticed the irons on Deacon's wrists and fell silent, his expression changing to surprise. 'Is this a joke?' he demanded.

'The sheriff's sins have caught up with him,' Logan said. 'Where are the cell keys?'

'In the right-hand drawer of the desk,' Deacon rasped. 'Walt, you can go off duty now. Drop into McSween's saloon and tell him I've been arrested.'

'Stay here,' Logan countermanded. 'What's your name, mister?'

'Roy Batley,' the jailer said. 'Who are you?'

'I'm Texas Ranger Travis Logan. As of this moment I'm running the law around here. Get the cell keys and we'll put my prisoners behind bars.'

Batley opened the drawer in the desk and produced the keys to the cells. He scurried through a door in the back wall of the office and Logan urged Deacon and Foster to follow. They entered the cell block, and Logan stood by with a levelled gun while Batley and locked both hapless lawmen in adjoining cells. Logan returned to the office with Batley in close attendance.

'I didn't see Smack Morgan in your cells,' Logan observed. 'He was wounded out at Tented H and Harlan was supposed to bring him in to be jailed.'

'I ain't seen hide nor hair of Morgan.' Batley shook his head. 'Maybe you should ask Deacon about it.'

'Later will do,' Logan said. 'What's the routine here for feeding the prisoners?'

'The hotel restaurant supplies us,' Batley said. 'I usually stop by there with an order and they deliver.'

'Do that now,' Logan said. 'And bring me something to eat; beef steak with all the trimmings, and plenty of coffee. And don't tell a soul the sheriff is behind bars. Do you know who usually rides in a posse? I'll need twenty men when I leave town later.'

'Sounds like you got a big load of

trouble to clean up,' Batley commented. 'I'll pass the word to Charlie Baine, the town mayor — he owns the Mercantile. He'll have a posse ready for you when you want it.'

'Take my horse with you and put it in the livery barn. Tell the stable man I'll need a fresh mount shortly. Arrange it for me, huh?'

'Leave it to me. I'll take care of everything.' Batley departed.

Logan sat down, trying to relax for the first time in many hours. He placed a pistol on the desk close to his right hand, put his elbows on the desk, and lowered his chin into his cupped hands to consider the situation. A stream of questions and conjecture flowed through his mind from the hectic experiences of the past twenty-four hours, and he sighed as he tried to pick out the most pressing of the leads he wished to follow up.

The throbbing of his wound brought him down to basics. If he didn't get his arm examined the wound could turn street door. The key was in the inside of the lock and he removed it. He left the office and locked the door, slipped the key into his pocket, and crossed the street to the doctor's house. Doc Keeble was not at home, but his wife was.

Mrs Keeble was a short, stout woman with greying hair and a motherly expression on her lined face. She took one look at Logan's bloodied arm and led him into the doctor's office, pushed him into a chair, and picked up a pair of scissors to cut away Logan's shirt sleeve. She tut-tutted when she saw the wound.

'This was done some time ago,' she observed. 'You should have come here sooner. The wound is already beginning to turn bad. I am a trained nurse so I can handle it. Just sit there quietly and I'll get a bowl of hot water.'

Logan closed his eyes, fighting against exhaustion and the desire to sleep. Mrs Keeble returned and set about cleansing the wound. Logan bore her ministrations silently, and when she had finished he thanked her and got to his feet.

'When the doc gets back, tell him to come and see me over at the law office. I'm Travis Logan, a Texas Ranger. I need to talk to him about some trouble that's coming here in town, and he will have to prepare for his side of it.'

He went out to the street and paused to look around. A rider was coming towards him, leading a pack horse, and he dropped his hand to his right-hand gun when he recognized Tom Barden. He recalled seeing Barden going into the outlaws' gorge the day before, and he watched the man turn into an alley next to McSween's saloon. His tiredness forgotten, Logan went across the street and hurried along the opposite sidewalk. It was time he started arresting his suspects; that was a part of the job he liked . . .

8

Logan entered the alley beside the saloon and hurried along to the back lots. He emerged from the alley and saw Barden leading his horses into a fenced yard where a couple of freight wagons were standing with their shafts pointing skywards. He went forward purposefully, his hand close to the butt of his right-hand gun. Barden took the two horses into a stable within the compound. Logan stepped into the doorway. He watched Barden unsaddle his horse and remove the freight frame from the second animal. Barden did not notice Logan until he turned to leave the stable, and halted abruptly when his gaze fell upon the Ranger, standing motionless. He reached for his holstered gun with surprising speed.

Logan flowed into action. His right-hand pistol came fast and smoothly into his hand and levelled at the third button on Barden's brown shirt. Barden halted his draw with his muzzle still in the holster. He thrust the weapon deep into leather and removed his hand from the butt.

'You surprised me, Ranger,' he said. 'You shouldn't oughta sneak up on a man that way. You might have got yourself shot. What can I do for you? Did you catch up with those two badmen you were following?'

'No, but I expect to see them soon. I want to talk about your movements over the last twenty-four hours. I saw you entering the gorge where Dolan and his gang are hiding out. I followed you in and watched you consorting with the outlaws. Dolan was waiting for the supplies you toted in. You and Larter have got a good trade going there. When do you expect Larter back from Buffalo Crossing?'

Barden moistened his lips. His face had stiffened as he heard Logan's

sive movement back to his holstered gun, but he thought better of it and dropped his hand to his side.

'You must have got me mixed up with someone else,' he said haltingly. 'I don't have any dealings with outlaws.'

'There's no mistake. You've got the kind of face a man can't overlook. I saw you on the trail with Larter, and hours later you turned up at the outlaw hideout, leading a pack horse; the one I saw tied to the back of Larter's freight wagon when I stopped you on the trail to ask about two outlaws. Don't deny it, Barden. I've got you dead to rights, and I heard you talking to Dolan. That clinches it for me, so I'm arresting you on the suspicion that you are dealing with known outlaws. Get rid of any weapons you've got on you, and be careful how you do it. I'm hair-triggered.'

Barden remained motionless for a moment, staring bleakly into Logan's taut features, and then he sagged a little

166

and took his pistol from its holster, using thumb and forefinger only. He dropped the weapon on the ground and raised his hands.

'You know where the jail is, so head for it, and keep your hands raised,' Logan said.

Barden began walking, making for the alley beside the saloon. Logan followed him, his gun down at his side. He saw two figures standing at the open back door of the saloon, and a warning sounded in his mind.

'Keep to the back lots and use the alley beside the law office,' Logan directed. 'Who are those two men at the saloon?'

Barden glanced to his right, took in the figures, and laughed harshly.

'They are friends of mine. The big guy is Bull McSween. The other one is McSween's saloon manager, Mike Banham.'

Logan studied the two men, who were gazing intently at Barden. McSween was a gross heavyweight normal sized men could fit comfortably into it. In addition to his great girth, McSween stood several inches over six feet. Everything about him looked larger than life. He was gigantic. His arms and legs were thick and powerful, his head much bigger than average, and his face looked like a full moon, fleshy, and giving the impression that he had stopped an inordinate number of blows with his nose and eyes over a long period of time. By contrast, Mike Banham was slim, and stood shorter than his boss by a good twelve inches.

Both men began to move along the back lots in the direction Logan and Barden were taking. Barden laughed.

'Looks like you've got trouble coming up, Ranger,' he said. 'McSween ain't the kind of man who watches while his friends are being arrested and dumped in jail, and he's a particular friend of mine.'

'If he breaks the law he'll find himself

in jail beside you,' Logan replied.

McSween had a peculiar gait. As he walked he rolled his shoulders from side to side and threw his weight forward, kicking his feet out as each thick leg reached the limit of its swing. His mouth was agape, as if the exercise was making him breathless. As they converged, Logan saw more details of the mountainous man. McSween was dressed in immaculate town clothes and shiny ankle-length boots. He had a cartridge belt buckled around his fleshy middle, and his ponderous right arm was bent, his large hand grasping the butt of the holstered pistol.

'Hey, hold up there, Barden,' McSween shouted in a deep voice that sounded like gravel rolling around in a barrel. 'Where are you going? Who is the guy behind you with the gun in his hand? Are you in some kind of trouble, Tom?'

'I'm being arrested by a Texas Ranger,' Barden replied.

done?'

Logan noticed that Banham was gripping his gun butt. He tensed for trouble.

'I ain't done a blamed thing against the law,' Barden said. 'I reckon it's a case of mistaken identity.'

'You two better change your minds about your intentions,' Logan warned sternly. 'Barden is my prisoner and I'm putting him behind bars. Don't get in my way.'

'Where's the sheriff?' McSween demanded. 'Why ain't he handling this?'

'He's in jail, and he'll be there a long time,' Logan retorted. 'Now stand aside and I'll go about my lawful business. Obstruct me in any way and you'll pay a full measure for going against the law.'

McSween glanced back towards the saloon and Logan looked in the same direction. He saw two other men emerging from the open back door and come hurrying towards them. Both newcomers were holding weapons.

'You'd better warn off your men, McSween,' Logan rapped. 'Barden is under lawful arrest, and nobody is gonna take him away from me. Are you prepared to take the law into your own hands? I'm ready to shoot anyone who tries.'

McSween grinned, his fleshy face creasing. 'You've got a suspicious mind, Ranger,' he said. 'What makes you think I'd go up against the law? I'm all for law and order, and if Barden has done something wrong then he'll have to face the consequences.'

'Then get to hell out of here!' Logan's patience was fast becoming exhausted. 'You've got five seconds to turn and walk away. After that I'll start shooting.'

McSween looked down at Logan from his great height and decided he was not bluffing. He threw his weight into motion, moved his feet quickly to maintain his balance, and turned away to start back to the saloon.

Banham. 'There's nothing for us here.'

'You can't walk away from me, McSween,' Barden shouted. 'I'm in trouble and you've got to do something. Larter will be back from Buffalo Crossing in a few days, and he'll raise hell if he finds me behind bars. Take care of this Ranger. He's only one man. He won't be missed. Kill him and throw him in the sink hole. There's a lot at stake, remember. If you let him put me behind bars I'll tell him about what's been going on around here, and if I do no one will be safe. I'll shout it to the mountains. Think on that, and do something before it's too late.'

The two men coming from the saloon reached McSween and words passed between them. Then all four men turned swiftly, reaching for their guns. Logan waited until he was certain of their intentions, and then drew both his guns. McSween was fast on the draw and his pistol came up into the aim with only one target in mind:

Logan. But Logan got off the first shot, and saw the strike of his slug. The bullet took McSween in the upper chest. The big man rocked back on his heels, but his pistol continued to lift.

Logan dropped to one knee and worked both pistols, shooting alternately. Banham cleared leather and was coming up into the aim. The other two men were buying into it. Logan triggered his weapons and hot lead slammed into the group. He worked his guns, throwing lead fast.

Amidst the drum-fire roll of gun thunder, McSween took a second bullet in the chest. He reared back like a nervous horse, dropped his gun and clutched at his chest. He lost balance and fell against Banham, taking him to the ground in a flurry of twitching arms and legs. Logan shifted his aim and triggered his pistols, cutting down the other two men before they could get into their stride. Banham fell clear of McSween and pushed to his feet, gun lifting. Logan shot him dead centre.

fell backwards, blood spouting from his throat.

In a matter of life-taking split-seconds it was over. Gun echoes fled across the town as Logan looked around for Barden. The freighter was fleeing for an alley mouth. Logan fired a shot over his head and Barden swung around, saw McSween and his three men down on the ground, and threw up his hands quickly in token of surrender. He came to Logan's side with his hands raised, his face expressing shock.

'Get down on the ground on your belly, put your hands out above your head, and don't move until I tell you,' Logan rapped. 'I want to check out your pards.'

Barden went down quickly and remained motionless. Logan went to where McSween was stretched out. He had fired six rapid shots. Two had struck McSween in the chest, but the big saloon man was still breathing, his immaculate shirt drenched in blood.

Banham was dead and the two unknown men were both seriously wounded. The echoes of the shooting were fading into the distance.

A man stuck his head out of the open back door of the saloon, attracted by the shots. Logan called and beckoned to him and, after hesitating, the man came hurrying forward. Logan shouted at him as he drew closer: 'Fetch the doctor. There are three injured men here. Make it quick.'

The man half turned and ran into the nearest alley. Logan called to Barden to get to his feet, and they continued to the jail. Barden was badly shocked by the shooting, which had not ended as he desired. Logan unlocked the door of the office and they entered.

'Sit down in front of the desk,' Logan said, and Barden slumped on the seat. Logan sat behind the desk and placed his pistol on the desktop, under his right hand. 'The action is over for now,' Logan continued, 'so let me hear what you've got to say. You told McSween going on around town. I'm listening, so start working your mouth.'

Barden shook his head. 'That was just talk. I thought McSween could take you.'

'That's what he thought.' Logan suppressed a sigh. 'Don't waste my time, Barden. I'll get at the truth anyway so you might as well start spouting what you know, and it might make the law go easy on you if you're not too involved.'

'I won't fall for that one,' Barden said harshly. 'I wasn't born yesterday.'

The street door opened and Batley, the jailer, entered the office. He gazed at Barden.

'I heard shooting while I was in the hotel,' he said. 'Was Barden involved?'

'Not directly,' Logan said. 'Lock him in a cell. He doesn't feel like talking at the moment, so we'll try him again after he's spent a few hours behind bars.'

'The grub will be along here as soon as it's cooked.' Batley took the cell keys out of the desk drawer, drew his gun, and ushered Barden out of the office.

Logan took time out to reload his guns. The street door was opened as he holstered the weapons and a tall thin man stepped in over the threshold. He had a shocked expression on his long face, and his brown eyes were wide and troubled. His light blue store suit hung on his frame. He came to the desk with quick, nervous steps and sat down on the chair recently vacated by Tom Barden.

'I assume you're Logan, the Texas Ranger,' he said in a high-pitched voice. 'I'm Charlie Baine, the town mayor. I own the Mercantile. Batley came and saw me a few minutes ago about forming a posse, and I'm here to do what I can to help. But I was told about the shooting on the back lots near the freighting depot — one man killed and three wounded, one of them a prominent member of this community. I went to look, and it was like something out of the war. I'm wary of forming a posse if for human life.'

'I want the posse as soon as possible,' Logan said in a firm tone. 'I know where the gang of outlaws responsible for most of the trouble around here is hiding out, and I want to put them out of action. I'm a lawman, Baine, a Texas Ranger, and I have a high regard for human life — that of honest, law abiding folks. The shooting on the back lots was not of my choosing. I had arrested Tom Barden on suspicion of dealing with outlaws, and he called on McSween and three others to help him. They drew their guns and I cut loose at them in defence of my life. Only one of the four was killed, and I'd say that was pretty good shooting. So what's your complaint? Do you have sympathy for wrong-doers?'

'I certainly do not! There will be an inquiry into the incident, and a copy will be sent to Ranger Headquarters.'

'That's fine.' Logan nodded. 'Just so long as you organize a posse for me before you do anything else. I want to be riding out in about an hour, and I reckon I'll need twenty posse men to handle the chore I have in mind. Can I rely on your co-operation?'

Baine heaved a sigh. He gazed at Logan's impassive face for several moments before nodding.

'The posse will be ready to ride whenever you want it,' he declared. 'But are you certain that Tom Barden has been breaking the law?'

'I wouldn't have arrested him if I didn't have proof.' Logan picked up the cell keys. 'Give me a moment and we'll talk to Barden. He's not ready to admit his guilt, but he'll come round after a day or two behind bars.'

Logan went into the cell block and unlocked the door of Barden's cell. He drew his right-hand gun.

'Come on, Barden,' he said, 'into the front office. We'll have another talk.'

'I ain't gonna open my mouth until I've seen Morris the lawyer,' said Barden stubbornly.

office. Baine got up from his seat in front of the desk and Barden slid into it. Logan sat down behind the desk, holding his pistol pointing at his prisoner.

'I saw Barden enter a gorge where a gang of outlaws were hiding,' Logan said. 'He was leading a pack horse loaded with supplies for them. I saw him in a shack talking to the gang boss, Walt Dolan, and from what I overheard I am certain Barden is in cahoots with the gang. I didn't get the chance to arrest him until I saw him coming into town a short time ago, and that was when McSween and three other men drew guns on me in an attempt to free Barden. Is that the truth of your arrest and the shooting, Barden?'

'That's roughly what happened,' Barden muttered. 'But it ain't true that I was taking supplies to the outlaws.' He paused and shook his head. 'Willingly, that is. The gang stopped me on the trail a couple of weeks ago. They stole what supplies I had, and threatened to kill me if I didn't take more stuff out to their hideout, which was what I was doing when you saw me. I had to do what they said. I ride some lonely trails around the county, and they could have dropped on to me at any time and carried out their threat to kill me.'

'That's not a good reason for helping outlaws,' Baine cut in. 'Why didn't you report to the sheriff? You could have got protection from the law.'

'Sheriff Deacon is behind bars,' Logan said. 'I've got proof that he is in with the outlaws.'

Baine remained silent, shocked by the revelation.

At that moment the street door swung open and two men lunged in across the threshold. Logan saw guns in their hands and threw himself sideways out of his chair, instinctively cocking his pistol. He hit the floor, and his injured arm took the impact. Pain shot through the limb, but he was intent on getting in the first shot and lunged to his feet.

newcomers, and he sidestepped to his right to get a clear shot. The next instant the office was rocked by rapid detonations as shooting erupted . . .

9

Logan moved back from the desk and dropped to one knee, his gun ready to fire. A bullet slammed into the top of the desk and two more just missed him. He saw Baine sprawling sideways, arms outflung, face contorted by shock and pain. As the town mayor fell, Logan was just able to see the head of the taller gunman behind Baine and triggered his pistol, adding to the gun thunder. Baine thudded to the floor. Logan's bullet struck the gunman in the face and he went down in a welter of flying blood.

The other gunman was intent on firing as many shots as possible. It was wild shooting — slugs ripped through the desk, hammered into the wall at the back of the office — but, in that first furious moment of action, Logan was not touched. His gun lifted, the muzzle seeking a target, and he waited a vital man before shooting.

The bullet struck the man in the chest and he went over backwards, still firing his gun until the hammer clicked on a spent cartridge. Logan got to his feet, his throat clogged with gunsmoke. Both men were out of action, and he walked around the desk to check them. They were dead. Logan turned his attention to Baine. The mayor was lying face down, blood spreading on his jacket behind his left shoulder.

Barden had not moved on his seat. He was staring at the two dead badmen, his mouth agape, lips moving silently as if he were praying. He moistened his lips, looked up at the grim-faced Logan, and gasped in a strangled tone.

'That's Hank Tolliver, one of Dolan's gang! They came to get me!'

'Dolan's gang?' Logan repeated. 'Are you sure about that?'

'Of course I'm sure!'

The street door was pushed open and

Logan turned with lifted gun, saw the newcomer was the jailer, and held his fire. Batley was holding a gun, and he holstered the weapon, his face expressing shock and excitement. He started asking questions, and Logan held up a hand, cutting off his excited flow.

'Get the undertaker in here and have the bodies removed. But get Doc Keeble first. The mayor looks to be in a bad way.'

Batley turned and hurried out of the office. Logan bent over the two unknown men and searched them, removing the contents of their pockets. He found nothing that would aid him to identify them. The door opened again and a man peered into the office. Logan dropped a hand to his gun but the man did not appear to be armed. He was tall and thin, with sharp features and pinched lips. He gazed at the two dead men, and gasped when saw the town mayor stretched out, still unconscious and bleeding.

'I'm Billy Grey,' he said, 'from the

cart out here.'

'Bring it in,' Logan said eagerly.

'What happened here?' Grey demanded.

'Ask me when I've eaten,' Logan replied. He motioned to Barden and pointed to the cell block with his pistol. Barden staggered to his feet and lurched forward. Logan locked him in his cell and went back into the office.

Grey brought in a large metal container and stood it on the desk. Steam rose when he removed the lid. He fetched in a wicker basket containing plates and utensils. Doc Keeble pushed open the door, and sniffed with appreciation as he came into the office, but went immediately to the inert mayor.

'I need to eat,' Logan said. 'How are McSween and those others?'

'They'll live. I've still got some work to do on McSween. You'll have to take them in here because I'm running out of room at my place.' He dropped to one knee beside Charlie Baine and made a cursory examination. 'I'll get some help to take Charlie over to my office.' He left his medical bag on the floor beside the unconscious town mayor and departed.

Two minutes later, Batley returned with a fleshy, greying, middle-aged man dressed in a black suit. He was small, his face expressionless.

'This is Mort Chandler, the undertaker,' Batley introduced.

Bill Grey laid a table cloth on the desk and set out the meal Logan had asked for. Logan began to eat hungrily, and Batley helped Grey take the rest of the food into the cells for the prisoners. The undertaker departed, muttering about fetching a cart to move the bodies. Doc Keeble returned with three men and Baine was lifted and carried out. When Batley came back into the office, Logan broached the subject of a posse.

'I'll go talk to Ben Farrant. He runs the gun shop along the street, and he's with a posse. He'll know the regulars, and he'll get them together ready to ride when you want them.'

Logan ate his meal and felt better for it. He drank two cups of coffee, and then sat back and began to think about taking out the posse. He was under pressure. The sheriff's fall from grace had added greatly to his problems. There were points he needed to check on but the menace of Dolan's gang hung over him like a shroud. He was tired, but the threat of the gang would not go away by itself. He had to go out and tackle it, and at this thought, a trickle of anticipation came to life in his breast.

The street door opened quietly, and Logan reached for his gun. He thrust it back into his holster when he saw Dinah Shadde. She was smiling wanly until she saw the two dead men lying on the floor. She halted and put her hands to her face. Logan got to his feet and went around the desk to her side.

He took her gently by the shoulder and led her out to the street.

'I'm sorry you saw that,' he said. 'I'm waiting for the undertaker to remove them.'

'I hope I'm not disturbing you,' she said hesitantly. 'I need to thank you for what you did when Cole was shot. You saved our lives and I am very grateful.'

'How is Cole?'

'Doc Keeble says he'll pull through, and it's all thanks to you. I dread to think what would have happened to me if you hadn't come along when you did. I've been hearing bits and pieces about what you've done since you brought us to town. There's so much trouble around here, and I thought it was only us being picked on.'

'Don't worry about any of it,' Logan advised. 'I've started cleaning up, and pretty soon there'll be no more badmen around.'

'You've been hurt,' she observed. 'Don't you have any help?'

He smiled. 'I'm used to working on

that what I do helps people like you and your husband. Thank you for dropping by.'

She smiled and reached out to grasp his right hand.

'Shall I see you back to where you are staying?' he asked.

She heard the sound of a cart on the street and glanced over her shoulder to see Mort Chandler arriving to collect the bodies in the office. She shuddered and turned away.

'God be with you,' she said as she hurried away.

Logan felt an unaccustomed thrill of emotion stab through him as he watched her walking along the street. It warmed him and strengthened his resolve. He saw Batley returning, chatting to the undertaker, and cut his thoughts short as he went back into the office.

Batley gave Chandler a hand to remove the bodies. When they were alone, Logan asked:

'What about the posse?'

'Farrant said he'd have it ready and waiting at the stable in half an hour.'

Logan nodded. 'Go to the store and get me a sack of supplies — enough to last three days. You're being a great help, Batley.'

'I'm glad you appreciate my efforts.' Batley grinned and departed once more.

Logan checked his guns; reloaded empty chambers. He was tired, but there would be no sleep for him this night. He was looking forward to facing the outlaws once more and bringing their criminal activities to an end. He mused over the situation until Batley returned, carrying a sack of supplies.

'Can you handle the jail and the prisoners while I'm out with the posse?' Logan asked.

'We have two stand-by jailers for when we get busy with prisoners. I'll have Bart Rogan in to help me until you get back. We'll manage.'

'I'll get moving then. I want to be in

Don't take any chances with the prisoners. Deacon will bust out if you give him half a chance.'

'They'll all be here when you get back,' Batley assured him. 'Good luck.'

Logan took his sack of supplies and left the office, then walked through the gathering shadows to the livery barn at the end of the street. There was movement within, and as he entered, he dropped his right hand to the butt of his gun. Three men were inside, saddling horses, and they turned to face him. One of them, a tall, thin individual with sharp features and narrowed eyes, smiled at him.

'I'm Ben Farrant,' he declared. 'Batley called on me to form a posse. Are you the Ranger?'

'Travis Logan. How many men have you got?'

Farrant shook hands with Logan. 'There'll be more than twenty by the time we're ready to ride.' He had a confident manner and looked reliable.

'I'm after the Dolan gang,' Logan told him. 'If they don't make a run for it and we can get at them before sunup we'll have a good chance of cleaning up.'

'Let's hope you're right,' Farrant said. 'They've sure been causing a lot of trouble around here. Is it true the sheriff is behind bars?'

'I arrested him, but no charges have been made yet.' Logan found his horse in a stall and saddled it.

Men began to arrive, solid, determined townsmen, well-armed and intent on what they had to do. There was some joking among them as they prepared to ride out, but mostly they were quiet. When Farrant told him the men he had selected were all present and ready, Logan spoke to them in a confident voice.

'We're going after the Dolan gang. If we can surround them then we'll get the drop and clean them out. I don't expect them to surrender, so if they fight then show them no mercy. They heading for a horse ranch to the north of Wadham's SW spread. Ben Wadham and some of his outfit are trailing in a herd of rustled cows the outlaws were moving out of the county, and I hope we'll meet up with them before the shooting starts.'

They led their horses out of the stable and mounted, moving quietly as night began to close in, and left the town resolving to end the trouble blighting their lives. Logan glanced back along the street as they hit the darkening trail, saw lamplight showing at some windows, and straightened his shoulders as he went forward. The weight of responsibility was heavy upon him and his thoughts were remote as they rode into the wilderness on a trail intended to lead them into hot action before next the sun showed . . .

Long hours passed. The posse rode steadily through the night, silent for the most part, minds fixed on the coming dawn. The moon showed later, giving silvery light to relieve the blackness of the range. They stopped regularly to rest their mounts. Peacefulness surrounded them — grim, law-abiding men determined to fight the badmen — pushing the eternal struggle between good and evil. They were familiar with the range. Farrant rode beside Logan at the head of the posse, and they were silent until Farrant said:

'We're about two miles from the horse ranch, Logan.'

'Good. There should be a rustled herd around here somewhere, and the SW outfit trailing it will be alert. Better tell the men to be wary. We don't want any accidents.'

Within minutes someone reported hearing a steer bawling. Logan called a halt.

'I'll go on ahead and try to find Ben Wadham,' he said to Farrant. 'There'll be some outlaws with the cattle and I don't want to arouse them before we're ready.'

The posse dismounted. Logan rode

Presently a low voice challenged him. He gave his name, his voice sounding husky, his hand ready to draw his gun should he have come across the rustlers. But Ben Wadham replied, giving his name, and Logan swung wearily out of his saddle. Wadham came out of the shadows.

'Have you got a posse with you?' he demanded.

'More than twenty men,' Logan replied.

'That's better than I expected. The cattle are settled down for the night. There are rustlers watching them. We can soon overpower them, but any shots we fire will be heard by the gang at the horse ranch and likely stampede the herd. I set Chuck Farris to watch the ranch with orders to come and tell me if the outlaws show signs of moving. So far I ain't heard from him so I reckon they haven't been alerted.'

'I need to scout around the ranch,' Logan said. 'But I intend putting the posse in position around the place to stop the outlaws if they do make a break for it. Come with me to where the posse is waiting so you'll know where it is, and then you can get your men in to join up with it.'

He retraced his steps and Ben Wadham accompanied him. Farrant emerged from cover. Logan left them talking, mounted his horse, and rode towards the ranch. He took a circuitous route, able to see to a fair distance in the uncertain moonlight. He circled the herd, shapeless shadows lying on the ground, and saw a nighthawk riding around the resting animals, singing softly to soothe them.

When he saw the stark outlines of the ranch he halted and tethered his mount in good cover, drew his rifle from its scabbard, and moved in towards the buildings. Tension filled him. He moved slowly and silently, gained the fence around the yard, and crouched to observe his surroundings. He didn't doubt there was a guard somewhere wondered what had happened to Chuck Farris.

The spread was not in complete darkness; lamplight shone from a front ground floor window. There was no sound to betray the presence of some twenty outlaws. Logan heard a horse stamp in the corral, but it was a natural sound. He closed in, circling the perimeter of the yard, needing to complete a circuit of the area before fetching in the posse.

He reached the rear of the house, sneaked in closer, moving cautiously. His mouth was open and he breathed shallowly, ears strained for sound, eyes watching his surroundings, looking for the presence of a prowling guard. He gained the wall of the house without incident and flattened against it, peering around. When he was satisfied that he had not alerted any guards he moved around the back corner, passed the kitchen, and rounded the far rear corner to move to the front of the house. The thought of the lighted window drew him like metal to a magnet.

When he reached the porch he kept out of the patch of lamplight on it and eased in towards the window. He could hear voices from inside the room and risked a quick glance at the interior, ducking back instantly. Dolan and a couple of outlaws were inside, standing in a tight circle around a man sitting on a chair, wrists lashed together, legs outstretched, and head lolling back. His eyes were closed, and there was blood on his face. Logan risked another look inside, and remained peering through the bottom corner of the glass. He recognized the seated man — had seen him with Ben Wadham when he and his outfit had arrived outside the deserted hideout in the gorge.

Farris was in bad trouble. Dolan was talking, and although Logan could hear the outlaw's strident voice he could not make out what was being said. When Farris did not respond to Dolan's front of his shirt and dealt him several hard punches to the face.

Logan clenched his teeth. He cocked his gun, moved along the porch, and paused outside the door. He could not leave Farris a prisoner of the outlaws. He had to free him before turning the posse on the gang.

He tried the door and it opened to his touch. He thrust it wide and lunged across the threshold. The three outlaws looked up quickly at his appearance and instinctively reached for their holstered guns.

'I'll kill the first man that touches a gun,' Logan rapped.

The two outlaws froze, staring at Logan's levelled gun, but Dolan continued his play, clearing leather despite the command. Logan leapt forward and struck Dolan's gun hand with his pistol barrel. Dolan's gun flew out of his hand. He cursed and lifted his hands to grapple with Logan, who swung his pistol in a back-handed blow and slammed it into Dolan's face. Dolan went down, spitting blood, and Logan straightened and covered the remaining two outlaws. Both were again reaching for their guns.

'Hold it,' Logan said. 'Get rid of your guns, one at a time.'

The outlaws forgot about resisting and disarmed themselves, dropping their weapons to the floor. Dolan was lying on his back, his hands covering his face, blood dribbling through his fingers. Logan, gun covering the outlaws, called to Farris, hunched in the chair.

'Farris, can you hear me? I'm Logan, the Texas Ranger. I need your help. Can you get up and join me?'

Farris straightened in the seat and opened his eyes. There were bruises on his face and his nose looked as if it were broken. He was dazed by the rough treatment he had suffered, but when he looked around the room, saw Dolan down and the other two outlaws standing with their hands shoulder pick up one of the discarded pistols.

'Let me kill Dolan,' he grated, covering the gang boss with the pistol.

'Cut that out,' Logan replied. 'I've got a lawful posse outside, not a mob. We'll try and get these three out of here, and then I'll call in the posse. We'll surround the place; I'll give the outlaws a chance to surrender, and if they won't then we'll attack them. There's a lariat on the wall over the fireplace — get it and tie these three.'

'You'll never get away with it,' Farris said angrily. 'Let's kill them while we have the chance. They are saddle-scum. They deserve all they get.'

'If you don't change your attitude, I'll disarm you and place you under arrest,' Logan said harshly. 'What's it to be?'

Farris glared at Logan for several moments, then went to the fireplace and picked up the rope. He holstered the gun he had picked up, produced a knife, cut lengths of rope off the coil, and proceeded to bind the three badmen while Logan menaced them with his pistol. Dolan began to protest as he was being bound. Logan stepped in behind the gang boss and struck him a single blow to the head that made Farris grin as he finished the task of binding Dolan.

Logan nodded when Farris had completed the chore. 'Now let's get them out of here,' he said. 'We'll take them to the posse and leave them under guard, then come back here and finish the job I set out to do.' He gazed at the outlaws. 'I don't have to tell you what will happen if you make any sound while we are leaving.'

The outlaws did not reply. Dolan was stirring on the floor. Logan pulled him upright.

'Link them together with short lengths of rope,' he instructed, 'so they can't make a run for it in the night. When we leave, you lead the way and I'll cover them from behind.'

Farris obeyed. Then he led the way out of the house, threatening the without protest, Dolan staggering between the other two. Logan followed on their heels, and closed the door quietly behind him. They crossed the yard in silence and faded into the shadows . . .

10

Logan held the prisoners just outside the ranch gate while Farris went off into the darkness to collect his horse. When Farris returned, Logan led the way to where he had left his mount. Then they set out, leading their horses and walking behind the outlaws. Dolan soon began to stumble, and after he had fallen several times on the uneven ground, Logan spoke sharply to him.

'If you don't keep moving on your feet I'll shoot you in the leg and the other two will carry you,' he warned.

'You won't get away with this,' Dolan replied, but nevertheless he remained on his feet and they made steady progress through the shadows.

Logan kept glancing over his shoulder in the direction of the ranch, which remained silent, lost now in the night. He was revising the rough plan he had

had Dolan, and the gang would be lost without a leader. It gave him an edge, and he was content. A low voice suddenly challenged them from the shadows ahead, and Logan cocked his gun.

'Is that you, Logan? Declare yourself. I've got you covered.'

Logan recognized Ben Farrant's voice. 'It's Logan,' he replied. 'I found Farris at the ranch, and I've got Dolan and a couple of his gang as prisoners.'

Shadows appeared out of the night, holding guns, and the posse men swarmed around Logan and his party. Logan narrated the incident that had occurred.

'It was lucky I got there when I did,' he ended. 'Farris looked to be in a bad spot. Now let's get on. I want this done with by the time the sun comes up.'

'We haven't been wasting our time,' Farrant said. 'I scouted around the herd with a couple of the men and we picked up two night herders and found three more men in a camp some way off from the steers. We took them prisoner. All we've got to do now is catch that bunch at the ranch.'

Logan was happy with the situation. He told Farrant to arrange guards for the prisoners, and minutes later those men who would accompany him back to the ranch were tightening cinches and preparing to move out. Farrant told Farris to remain with the prisoners but Farris objected.

'I want to get at the outlaws,' he said. Farrant appealed to Logan, who shook his head.

'If he's so eager then let him come along with us,' he replied.

Farris joined the posse and they rode in the direction of the ranch, halting out of earshot of the spread. A man was detailed to look after the horses. Logan gave his final orders.

'Take half the posse,' he told Farrant, 'and cover the rear of the ranch. 'There are two horse lines beyond the barn, and from what I saw earlier, I think in the barn. You take up positions between the barn and their horses to cut them off and I'll take Ben Wadham and his outfit between the house and the barn and confront them. I'll give the gang a chance to surrender, but if they start shooting then pour it into them.'

'Give me ten minutes to get into place,' said Farrant in a grim tone.

They moved in closer and then split into two groups. Farrant went off into the shadows to the left of the ranch and Logan led his men along the right side of the house to the rear and they formed a rough line in the back yard between the house and the front of the barn. He told two men to watch the rear of the house. They settled down noiselessly.

Logan counted off the seconds. Their eyes had become accustomed to the night and they were able to see well enough in the starlight. When he judged that Farrant and his men were in position, he fired a shot skywards.

A string of echoes fled through the night, but there was no immediate reaction from the outlaws. Logan paused for long moments, and then shouted:

'Hello, you men in the barn. This is Travis Logan, Texas Ranger. I have a posse surrounding you. Come out with your hands up and surrender to the law. Walt Dolan is already under arrest.'

Logan's voice echoed around the yard. He heard posse men cocking their weapons. The front of the barn was windowless, the big doors closed. Nothing happened for what seemed an age, and then shooting erupted at the rear of the barn; a few isolated shots initially, and then a fusillade, rolling like rippling thunder.

The big barn doors were thrust open and several figures appeared, running to left and right in a desperate bid to get clear; guns hammered and muzzle flame distorted the shadows. Law guns replied raggedly, and the shooting fighting.

Logan fired both his guns, shooting at opposing gun flashes that burned holes in the shadows. His teeth were clenched, his eyes narrowed. Outlaws began falling in their tracks. Hot lead came whining back in answer. The racket of the guns seared through the night, rapid and desperate. The shooting reached a high note and was sustained. But it was a turkey-shoot! The running outlaws had no hiding place — had to run the gauntlet of indomitable posse men. Red muzzle-flame lanced the shadows; there was no way out. Suddenly there were no more figures in sight and the shooting dwindled until an uneasy silence settled and echoes faded away across the range.

'Do you know how many outlaws were here?' Ben Wadham demanded. He was kneeling beside Logan, his pistol cocked and covering the doors of the barn.

'No more than twenty-five,' Logan replied. 'We took three prisoners out of it, so we need a count of those that tried to escape both front and back to get a rough idea of how many were still around.'

'Leave it to me.' Wadham got to his feet and went across the yard.

Logan went forward, stuffing fresh shells into his empty chambers. He took up a position beside the open barn doors.

'Hey, inside the barn,' he called. 'Any more of you wanting to surrender can come out, hands up, minus weapons, and you'll be arrested. You've got two minutes to make up your minds before we come in after you.'

There was no reply, and tense moments passed. Ben Wadham came back to Logan. He was breathing heavily.

'There are seven outlaws down around here,' he reported. 'I checked with Farrant and he says he's counted six around the back. It looks like we got put out here while he goes into the barn to check.'

A burst of shots sounded inside the barn before Logan could reply. They waited, and presently Farrant's voice sounded, and lantern-light flickered inside the building.

'Logan, we got two more of them in here. They are dead. Hold your fire, we're coming out.'

Men emerged from the barn. Farrant came to Logan's side.

'That was short and sweet,' he observed. 'Bill Thompson and Ray Miller caught slugs, but they aren't seriously hurt.'

'Danny Boyd took a slug in his right shoulder,' Ben Wadham cut in.

'Let's check the house now,' Logan said. 'Farrant, take your men around to the porch and cover the front. We'll go in the back door and finish the job.'

The posse moved quickly. They entered the house. Boots thudded on wooden floors, voices shouted, and in a few short minutes it was reported that there were no outlaws around.

'Gather the dead men and put them in the barn,' Logan said. 'Bring any wounded into the house and we'll do what we can for them. Farrant, send some men to the herd and have those prisoners there brought to the house. Then we'll head back to town.'

The sky was lightening with grey dawn by the time the posse was ready to ride back to town, but the smell of frying bacon filled the ranch house as a couple of posse men, hungry after the swift action, decided they could not wait to get back to town. They all took time out for a meal.

'Riders are coming into the yard,' warned one of the guards Farrant had set to watch the approaches. 'Five of them,' he amended.

Logan went out to the porch, followed by several posse men. Lamplight issuing from the windows of the house slashed through the shadows. The riders came openly across the yard, strengthening daylight. Logan noted that they were not holding guns. He stepped down off the porch and moved forward a couple of paces, his right hand resting on the butt of his holstered gun.

'Declare yourselves,' he called.

'We're Tented H,' was the immediate reply. 'Harlan sent us over to collect the herd. He wants it moved out of the county. We'll trail it over to the railroad at Buffalo Crossing. Harlan is worried because Rangers are about.'

Logan could hear the surrounding posse men cocking their pistols. He drew his gun and eared back the hammer to full cock. The riders were now only twenty feet from the porch.

'Come on in,' he called. 'Don't reach for your guns. We're a posse from Alder Creek. We've got you covered.'

The newcomers halted abruptly, uttering cries of consternation, utterly surprised. For a moment there was silence and no movement. Then three

214

of the men raised their hands immediately, but two reached for their guns. The posse men cut loose instantly. The two men went out of their saddles. The remaining three sat motionless, hands raised high. Logan was elated. This was the law in operation, and it pleased him because Harlan had exposed his hand in this high-stakes game.

The posse men went forward and took their prisoners, disarmed them, bundled them into the ranch house. Logan confronted them. They were shocked, demoralized by the abrupt change of their circumstances. He recognized Smack Morgan, whom he had shot when he visited Tented H.

'Harlan was supposed to take you into town and put you behind bars,' Logan observed. 'When I got back to town and found you hadn't arrived, I wondered why he hadn't kept his word. Now I know why. You'll see the inside of the jail now, and Harlan will be with you shortly.'

town with his prisoners. The posse men were cheerful, relieved that the action was behind them. The prisoners were bound and pushed into saddles. Ben Wadham approached Logan as final preparations were being made.

'I reckon I should stay with the herd — start them towards SW. We can hold them on the ranch until the owners of the brands that were rustled can come and collect them.'

'That's a good idea,' Logan replied. 'You do that, Ben. I'm thinking of cutting away from this bunch now. The posse can handle the prisoners with no trouble, and I can ride to Tented H and pick up Harlan. With him in jail, I reckon the trouble will be over.'

'You can't ride alone!' Alarm sounded in Wadham's voice.

Logan smiled. 'I do most of my law dealing alone,' he said. 'Don't worry about me.' He spoke to Farrant. 'Can you get these prisoners back to town and put them behind bars?'

'Consider it done!' Farrant nodded emphatically. He turned and addressed the waiting posse men. 'Let's head for town,' he called. 'We'll put these skunks where they belong: behind bars.' He grinned at Logan. 'Good luck,' he said, and added doubtfully, 'I don't like the thought of you riding alone to Tented H. Why don't you take a couple of posse men with you?'

'I appreciate the thought, but I can do my job. The posse have done its duty, and now I have to do mine. When you get to town send the undertaker out here with a wagon to collect the bodies.'

Farrant nodded and turned away. He stepped up into his saddle and rode out at the head of his cavalcade. Logan stood in the yard and watched them go. Ben Wadham moved restlessly at his side.

'We'll be on our way now,' he said. 'I'll see you when you've cleaned out Tented H. I've always suspected Harlan was somehow involved in the trouble.'

him.

Wadham rode out of the yard with his outfit and headed for the waiting herd. Logan heaved a sigh and went to where he had left his horse. The sun was coming up above the horizon and the last vestiges of night were disappearing. Another day had dawned, and he was gripped by the feeling that he had broken the back of the trouble he had come to handle.

He rode out, grim-faced, his thoughts going over what he had accomplished and what was still to be done. He looked around, got his bearings, and rode in the direction of Tented H.

It was noon when he slid out of his saddle behind a ridge above Harlan's cattle spread. He got down and bellied up the slope until he could peer over the crest. The ranch was spread out before him and he studied the stark buildings. There was a guard at the gate, moving restlessly, a rifle in his hands. Two men were standing in the open doorway of the barn. A cowboy in the corral was breaking in a horse. It was a peaceful scene of a normal ranch going about its usual business.

Logan studied the house, where nothing moved, and wondered what Harlan was doing. He moved back to his horse, his mind already thrusting up his future moves. He needed to get to Harlan, arrest him, take him out of the ranch and away from his outfit, and put him in jail.

He had seen a draw cutting down a nearby slope of a ridge towards the ranch, ending some distance from the spread where the ground flattened out into rangeland. He moved back from the ridge until he found a good place to leave his horse knee-hobbled, took his rifle from is saddle scabbard, and filled his pockets with rifle shells from his saddle-bags. He reloaded the empty chambers of his pistols and thumbed pistol ammunition in the empty loops on his cartridge belts.

He entered the overgrown draw and

which faced the right side of the house with thirty yards of level ground between.

The front yard was to his right, the corral on his left, with the cook shack beyond it, close to the bunk house. The barn was behind the house. There was now no sign of the two men who had been standing in the doorway of the barn. Logan looked around and selected his route to pass behind the back of the cook shack. He decided to head for the rear of the barn, check inside for the two men he had seen there, and then cross the back yard to the rear door of the house to confront Harlan.

The wrangler had gone from the corral. As he neared the cook shack, Logan heard sounds within, and went to the door and pushed it open. An old man wearing an off-white apron was busy at the stove. He was tall and lean, bald, and his long face was wrinkled with age. He caught Logan's movement in the doorway and looked up quickly.

'Who in hell are you?' he demanded.

'I've ridden over from Dolan's hideout. I've got a message for Harlan, and he ain't in the ranch house.'

'You're damn right he ain't. He had me up in the middle of the night to give him breakfast, and he rode out before first light. Are you one of Dolan's gang?'

'I wouldn't ride in here with a message from Dolan if I wasn't. Where's Harlan gone?'

'Why ask me? I'm only the cook around here. Talk to one of the outfit, if you can find anyone. Five of them rode out to see Dolan. Did you meet them on the trail?'

'I saw them at the hideout before I left. They said something about relieving us of the rustled steers. So where's Harlan gone?'

'He said he was going into town. Someone showed up from Alder Creek with word that McSween is in jail, along with Sheriff Deacon. That Ranger; he's only one man, but he's

221

into town if you wanta talk to the boss today.'

'I'll do that. Don't burn the grub.' Logan turned to depart, and as he stepped outside a gun muzzle jabbed into his stomach. He looked into the narrowed eyes of one of the men he had seen standing in the doorway of the barn. Before he could move he was struck on the head with a heavy object by the second man at the opposite side of the doorway. The ground seemed to fly up towards him, and then his face smacked it. His senses fled . . .

The toe of a boot kicking him in the ribs brought him back to his senses. He looked up to see both men standing over him, covering him with their pistols. They were grinning, their eyes filled with the hard expression of the gunman despite their levity.

'Get up,' one of them said. He was short, running to fat; a well-worn Stetson hung down his back, suspended by its chin strap. His lank brown hair looked as if it hadn't been washed in months.

'You're the Texas Ranger everyone is talking about,' the other said. Lean as a rake, his taut features looked sinister with a white scar that ran from his left ear to the bridge of his long nose. 'They're saying you're hell on wheels! Well, you don't look tough to me. Let's go over to the house. Smack Morgan is there. You shot him in the shoulder on your last visit. He described you and told us to watch out for you. I wouldn't wanta be in your boots, Ranger. He's done nothing but talk about what he'll do when he gets his hands on you, and I'm curious to see what happens now you're here.'

Logan got to his feet and put his hands to his head. The ranch seemed to be swirling and tilting around him. He felt hands snatching his pistols from their holsters, and then a rough hand thrust him between the shoulder blades and he staggered across the yard in the direction of the house . . .

11

Logan stumbled on the porch step and fell to his hands and knees. The shorter of the hardcases had holstered his gun. He grasped Logan's shoulder and dragged him upright. Logan, watching alertly, noted that the man had inadvertently moved into the tall man's line of fire. Logan reacted instinctively, turning and grasping Shorty, moving behind him. His left arm slid around the man's neck and dragged him back off balance, his right hand dropping to the man's holstered gun.

His fingers closed around the butt and the pistol came free. Logan cocked the weapon as he levelled it. The man with the gun was taken by surprise; found himself staring into the black muzzle of Logan's pistol. Logan triggered a shot and the slug struck the man's gun hand. Shorty suddenly flared into action; he grasped Logan's left arm, which was around his neck, and exerted pressure. Pain seared through Logan's wound. He backed off, turning towards his left to ease the pressure on his arm. He swung his right arm in a vicious arc and the gun in his hand slammed against Shorty's skull.

Shorty dropped to the ground. Logan looked around and saw the other man facing him, blood dripping from his right hand, his gun gripped firmly in his left. The muzzle gaped at Logan, who was half-turned away. Logan froze and released his gun, and the noise it made hitting the ground sounded like a death knell.

'I got you dead to rights, Ranger,' the man snarled. He waggled his gun. 'You're standing on the brink right now, and I'm gonna push you straight into hell.'

'Don't shoot him, Frazee.' The voice came from the house. 'Bring him in here. I want the pleasure of sending him where he should be, but Harlan up we are to hold him until he gets back from town, so bring him in here.'

Logan saw a figure at a front window of the house and recognized Smack Morgan, who was holding a pistol in his right hand although his right shoulder was heavily bandaged.

'You heard the man,' Frazee said to Logan. 'Get along into the house.'

Logan obeyed, his teeth clenched, his mind turning over at speed as he tried to think of some way of regaining the initiative. But his captor stayed out of arm's length and, as he entered the house with his hands raised, Logan was aware that his luck had finally run out.

Morgan covered Logan with his gun when he entered the big room. The gunman's face was contorted with rage.

'I'd like nothing better than to send you to hell with a band playing,' Morgan snarled, 'but Harlan pays the wages, and he wants you personally. Hogtie him, Frazee, and then you and Ellis ride him into town. Harlan will

226

have taken over there by now, so get moving.'

Logan submitted to being tied — Morgan stayed well out of contact while Frazee bound him. Frazee became a man of action, and bustled Logan out to the porch. Ellis was sitting in the yard, his hands to his head, still dazed by the blow he had received.

'Come on, Ellis,' Frazee called. 'We got a job to do. Let's saddle up and head for town. We'll maybe get ourselves a drink when we hand this buzzard bait over to Harlan.'

Within a few minutes, Logan was roped to a horse and Ellis — still groggy — and Frazee were herding him out of the yard on the ride to town. Morgan stood on the porch watching them depart. Logan tried in vain to loosen the rope binding him, but the tough fibre was impervious to his attempts. They rode in silence towards the distant town, Logan leading the way. Ellis, at his side, was holding the reins of Logan's horse, and Frazee was neckerchief around his injured right hand.

Unable to get free of his bonds, Logan gave up trying, and set his mind to thinking about his position. He had to get free before they reached town, for he had no illusions about what would happen to him if he fell into Harlan's hands.

They rode at a lope, jogging along the trail at a gait which covered the miles effortlessly. Logan's head ached. He had forgotten the number of times he had been struck with a pistol. He gripped his mount with his knees, and desperation filled his mind as the miles slipped behind them. There was no way out of this situation. In all his experience he had always come up with an answer to the wiles of the badmen he hunted, but now he had to admit defeat, and he wished he had listened to Farrant about taking a couple of posse men along with him.

The empty trail seemed to mock him,

until he spotted a rider ahead, crossing the crest of rising ground. The next moment the rider disappeared over the crest and was gone from sight. Logan felt his small surge of hope dwindle. There was no one in this county, outside of town, who knew he was a Ranger. He could not expect help from anyone.

When he passed over the crest where he had seen the rider he looked around, hoping against hope that help was at hand. But the rider was nowhere in sight, and he glanced down at the trail, instinctively looking for tracks. He saw hoof prints in the dust, followed them with his keen gaze, and saw that they entered a cluster of rocks fifty yards ahead. The trail swung out around the rocks, and Logan saw nothing of the rider as he rode by.

His captors apparently saw nothing, or were not alarmed by the sight of a lone rider. They cleared the rocks, and then a high-pitched voice called out.

'Hold up there, you two men. I've got

up. I want to know why you've got Logan hogtied.'

Logan's hopes sank as he recognized the voice. It was female, and sounded like Loretta Wadham. He looked over his shoulder and saw her horse emerging from the cluster of rocks. She had a .38 Colt pistol gripped in her right hand, her face showing determination. He grimaced, afraid for her.

'That man holding the gun — get rid of it,' she said firmly. 'I told you to get your hands up so do it now or I'll start shooting.'

Ellis reined in, halting Logan's horse and lifting his hands higher than his shoulders. Frazee looked at Loretta and sneered.

'Are you loco, gal? We're a couple of posse men,' he bluffed, 'and Logan is our prisoner. Put your gun away and get out of here. We ain't in the mood for playing games.'

Loretta fired her pistol and Frazee's hat whirled off his head and fell into the dust. Frazee dropped his gun in shock and slowly raised his hands.

'That's better.' Loretta said. 'You better know that shooting your hat off your head was no fluke, mister. I can hit anything I point my gun at, and I ain't afraid to shoot polecats. Now you, fat man, untie the Ranger and let him take your gun. Be careful how you move — anything sudden and I'll shoot. Get to it.'

Logan uttered a silent prayer as Ellis untied him, and when he was free he snatched the gun out of Ellis's holster. His relief soared as he covered the two men.

'Dismount,' he ordered, and they did so with alacrity. Logan dismounted, his gun unwavering. 'You shouldn't be out here on a lonely trail, Loretta,' he observed.

'It's a good thing for you I was on my way to town to visit with Dinah Cole,' she replied. 'How'd you manage to get in such a fix?'

'You've saved my life,' he responded.

that. Thank you for being right here and now. But this isn't the time for an explanation. I have to get to town, and I suggest you put off your trip until another day. There's likely to be a lot of shooting when I get there.'

Her expression showed that she did not like what he said, but the set of his jaw warned her that argument would be useless.

'I'll go back home,' she said.

'And I'll come and see you when this is all over,' he replied.

'I'm so pleased I was able to help you.' She turned her horse and began riding back the way she had come.

Logan watched her out of sight, his gun unwavering, covering the two motionless badmen. When she had gone he turned, waving his gun.

'Shorty, hogtie your pard, and do a good job; I'll check your knots. Leave enough rope for yourself. I'll bind you. Then we'll get on. I've got a job to do.'

With both men securely bound, they

continued without further incident until the town appeared in the distance. Logan steeled himself for action. He had no idea why Harlan had come to town, but he knew that whatever he did, the crooked rancher would make life tough for him. He did not like to think of the trouble he would get if Harlan had busted the prisoners out of jail.

He decided to approach the law office from the rear, and so left the trail to circle the town. The back lots were deserted, and he urged his prisoners into the alley beside the jail and dismounted. He checked his prisoners, ensuring that they could not get loose, and then tied their reins to a convenient hook in the wall of the jail.

'If I hear any noise from either of you while I'm away then I'll come back and gut-shoot the pair of you,' he warned. 'Don't make any mistake about that and keep your traps shut.'

They did not reply. Logan turned away, drawing his gun. He went to the look around. The town was silent and still and it struck him that the scene was not natural. He walked to the door of the law office and it opened to his touch. He entered, nerves tense, not knowing what to expect, and he got a shock when he saw Abe Deacon seated at the desk as if he had never been arrested. The ex-sheriff was wearing a law badge.

Deacon looked up, and tensed when he recognized Logan.

'What are you doing out of your cell?' Logan demanded. As far as he could see, Deacon was not armed. 'Who let you out?'

'An old friend of mine,' Deacon replied. 'All your prisoners have gone, except for those nursing wounds. A trap has been set for you, Logan. You got into town easy-like, but wait until you try to leave. There's no way out for you, so why don't you put down your guns and give in?'

Logan said nothing. He drew his

left-hand gun and cocked it. Deacon grimaced.

'There are three men in the cell area, well-armed, and just waiting for you to open that door. No matter which way you came into town, you will have been seen, and now armed men are moving in around the jail to take you.'

'Are you armed?' Logan demanded.

'No. I'm certain you won't shoot an unarmed man. I'm here to tell you of the situation.'

'Sit still. Don't move a muscle.'

Logan moved to the front window, looked outside, and his breath hissed between his clenched teeth when he saw men on the street, converging on the law office. He holstered his left-hand gun as he moved back to the door to lock it. There was a thick wooden bar leaning against the wall at the side of the door and he picked it up and dropped it into the metal brackets on the door posts. He returned to the window, peered out; counted six men coming towards the

Logan lifted his pistol and smashed the window pane, thrust the muzzle into an aiming position and fired a shot into the street a foot in front of the advancing men.

The crash of the shot destroyed the silence. The men halted in a line and stood motionless, apparently awaiting orders. A voice called loudly, the speaker unseen.

'Is that you in the office, Logan? This is Harlan. Come on out with your hands up. You're outnumbered. You don't have a chance. I've got you cold.'

'And if I surrender you'll kill me,' Logan replied. 'Thanks, but no thanks. If you want me then come in and get me, Harlan — the hard way. But there is a better way of handling this. You and your men throw down your guns and surrender to me. That way no one will get hurt.'

A gun blasted and a pane of glass over Logan's head shattered. He moved to one side, drawing his second gun, and cocked both weapons. He glanced towards the desk. Deacon sat motionless, both hands in plain view, a half smile on his fleshy face. Before he could begin shooting a fusillade of shots hammered, and the rest of the front windows splintered and fell. Logan felt pain in his left cheek, lifted a hand, and saw blood on his fingers.

He triggered his guns, firing alternately. The men outside were in the act of running forward to get into cover by the front wall of the office. Logan's slugs raked them. Two fell instantly. He crouched, his guns ready for targets, and fired rapidly, dimly aware of bullets hammering into the office through the shattered windows.

He stepped to one side for cover, and saw Deacon in the act of going to the floor, his chair overturning. Bullets were gouging strips out of the desk and thudding into the back wall of the office, riddling the door leading into the cell area. He was amazed at the volume of fire smashing into the office; all he fire.

The shooting continued for long moments, wrecking the office. A rack of long guns — rifles and shotguns — was hit and fell off the wall under the lethal hail of lead. A mug standing on the desk suddenly jumped and flew into pieces. Woodwork was splintered. Nothing escaped the fire, and just when it seemed the racket would continue forever, it began to dwindle, until an uneasy silence prevailed and only fading echoes remained.

'Are you coming out, Logan?' Harlan called. 'There's plenty more slugs ready if you've a mind to be stubborn.'

'Go to hell!' Logan replied, thumbing fresh shells into his empty chambers.

'Shoot the hell out of him,' Harlan shouted to his gunmen, and the racket was resumed.

Logan dropped to one knee. The thick adobe front wall was absorbing the flying slugs, but he knew it was being chipped away by the fusillade. He kept an eye on the door leading into the cells, expecting the men through there to come storming into the front office with flaming guns. He saw Deacon lying inert on the floor, his face turned away from the wrecked front windows.

The shooting continued at a furious rate, but Logan noticed that the volume of fire coming into the office was diminishing, although the sound level did not drop. He frowned and stood up, peering outside. The street was almost deserted again, and he saw the gunmen were no longer shooting at him but aiming their shots along the street. He fired at them, his accurate fire sending them hunting cover. Then the shooting ceased abruptly, and silence returned. Logan waited stoically.

Moments later, a voice called again, and it wasn't Harlan's.

'Hello in the office. This is Ben Farrant out here with the posse. We've chased off the gun-hands. You can open the door now. Harlan and some of his men have gone into McSween's saloon.'

moment later Farrant stepped into view and came across the street towards the office, flanked by posse men. Logan went to the door, removed the bar, and turned the key in the lock. The door swung open. It was riddled with bullets. Logan turned and covered Deacon, but the crooked sheriff did not move.

Farrant appeared in the doorway, grinning widely. 'We heard the shooting when we got near to town so I left our prisoners on the trail with three men to cover them and brought the rest in at a run. We were fired at as we came by McSween's saloon, and I saw McSween at his batwings. I thought he was behind bars.'

'He was when we left town yesterday, but Harlan got word and came in with some of his outfit, busted open the jail, and turned the prisoners loose. Cover me while I take a look in the cell block. Deacon said there were three gunmen inside, waiting for me to put in an appearance, but I think he was bluffing.'

Farrant checked his pistol, reloaded three empty chambers from the loops in his cartridge belt, and crossed the office to the door leading into the cells. On his way, he paused beside Deacon, bent over him, and then looked up at Logan.

'He's dead,' he reported.

Logan made no comment. He went to the door to the cells and pushed it wide, his gun covering the interior. The cell block was almost empty — only half a dozen wounded men remained, except for Batley, the jailer, who was locked in a cell.

'Deacon was bluffing,' Logan said. He went back to the desk, picked up the cell keys, and freed Batley.

The small jailer emerged from the cell, shaking his head, looking shame-faced.

'I'm sorry, Logan, but I didn't have a chance when Harlan and his outfit came in. There were six of them.'

'Don't worry about it,' Logan

prisoners arriving shortly. Deacon is lying dead in the front office. Perhaps you'll take over again, huh?'

'Sure thing.' Batley started grinning.

Logan turned to the street door. 'It's time to head for the saloon and finish off this chore,' he said.

'I sent some men around to the back door of the saloon to cut off any badmen attempting to flee,' said Farrant, accompanying him. 'Three posse men are covering the batwings, so we've got them boxed in.'

'You're thinking like a lawman,' Logan told him.

'I've been out with a posse a great many times,' Farrant retorted.

They went out to the boardwalk. Several armed men were standing around, and they were posse men. Logan looked at the half dozen bodies strewn around the street in front of the office. Doc Keeble was already checking them. Logan started along the street, heading for McSween's saloon, and Farrant motioned for the posse men to join them.

There was no shooting from the saloon, although three posse men were watching it from across the street. Logan stopped short of the batwings.

'You'd better send some more men around to the rear,' he said, 'and cover the side windows in the alley.'

Farrant gave the order and some posse men turned off into the nearest alley. Logan went on to the front corner of the saloon.

'It's too quiet,' Farrant said. 'We'll get our faces shot off if we attempt to go in there.'

'I'll give them a chance to surrender,' Logan said.

Farrant laughed; an ugly sound. 'You lawmen,' he said, 'you're all the same. You get a bunch of crooks at your mercy, and instead of shooting the hell out of them you ask them to come out with their hands up. Let's pour some lead in at them and help them make up their minds about coming out.'

a cocked gun in his hand he edged towards the saloon window. Then he noticed a saddle horse standing on the street with trailing reins in front of the saloon, and a jolt of shock hit him when he recognized it as the animal Loretta was riding when she got the drop on his captors. He halted and gazed at the animal while his mind gyrated.

A sigh escaped him. What was her horse doing here? She had turned and apparently headed back to the SW ranch when he warned her of the impending trouble. He grimaced as the truth hit him: she had followed him again. His teeth clicked together as he assumed that she had somehow got caught up in the situation and had been taken into the saloon.

The thought of her being held by the badmen galvanized him into action. He drew his second gun, cocked it, and hurled himself through the batwings, diving for the floor, shooting rapidly as his appearance sparked the gunmen inside into furious action. He looked around quickly, saw Loretta towards the rear of the long room with McSween by her side, and concentrated on the men trying to kill him.

His guns blasted. This was what he was good at, the culmination of a deadly assignment. He was aware of slugs coming at him, of shooting at figures resisting him. Tables had been overturned and were being used as flimsy shields. He swung his guns, firing instinctively, aiming for figures rearing up to take him on. He felt a flash of pain in his right thigh, cut down the man who had shot him, and slipped into his deadly rhythm, his killing action.

He was dimly aware that Farrant had entered the saloon on his heels and was cutting loose at his side. He saw Frank Harlan over by the bar and turned his attention to the crooked rancher. Harlan was down on one knee, his mouth agape as if cursing, but his voice was lost in the overwhelming clamour and the rancher pitched sideways to the floor.

More posse men entered the saloon, guns racketing in the timeless action. Logan emptied his left-hand gun and thrust it back into his holster. He did not waste a shot. He felt a slash of red hot pain slice through his right hip, but kept shooting.

He looked for Loretta; he saw McSween pushing her towards a rear door, his gross figure menacing, his massive arm around Loretta's slim figure. Logan triggered his pistol, aiming at the big saloon man's right leg and the shot broke the limb. McSween went down like a tree uprooted in a hurricane. Loretta was flung sideways, and stayed down on the floor.

The shooting was diminishing. Some of the badmen were standing up and raising their hands. Logan surged to his feet, intending to go to Loretta's side, but his right leg refused to take his weight and he fell forward on his face.

He tried to rise once more but flopped back and lost his hold on his gun. Silence came uneasily. The long room, streaked with drifting gunsmoke, was suddenly filled with posse men.

Logan felt an increasing sense of lassitude assailing him. He stayed down, aware of pain seeping into his body. He wanted to go to Loretta, but his strength and determination was running out. He made a final effort to get up. There was so much he had to do. Then he saw Loretta coming towards him, and as she dropped to her knees beside him he stopped resisting the inevitable and relaxed into unconsciousness. As he slid into blackness he tried to retain the thought that something would have to be done about her habit of failing to obey an order . . .

reading this large print book.

Did you know that all of our titles are available for purchase?

We publish a wide range of high quality large print books including:
Romances, Mysteries, Classics
General Fiction
Non Fiction and Westerns

Special interest titles available in large print are:
The Little Oxford Dictionary
Music Book, Song Book
Hymn Book, Service Book

Also available from us courtesy of Oxford University Press:
Young Readers' Dictionary
(large print edition)
Young Readers' Thesaurus
(large print edition)

For further information or a free brochure, please contact us at:
Ulverscroft Large Print Books Ltd.,
The Green, Bradgate Road, Anstey,
Leicester, LE7 7FU, England.
Tel: (00 44) **0116 236 4325**
Fax: (00 44) **0116 234 0205**